8 24 09

GRAVE FOR A
DEAD GUNFIGHTER

Other westerns by Kent Conwell:

GRAVE FOR A
DEAD GUNFIGHTER

•

Kent Conwell

AVALON BOOKS
NEW YORK

Published by Thomas Bouregy & Co., Inc.
160 Madison Avenue, New York, NY 10016

Library of Congress Catologing-in-Publication Data

Conwell, Kent.
Grave for a dead gunfighter / Kent Conwell.
    p.   cm.
ISBN 978-0-8034-9910-2   (acid-free paper)
I. Title.

PS3553.O547G73   2008
831'.54—dc22
                                    2008005921

PRINTED IN THE UNITED STATES OF AMERICA
ON ACID-FREE PAPER
BY HADDON CRAFTSMEN, BLOOMSBURG, PENNSYLVANIA

To my grandson, Keegan, and to Amy and Jason who by now are well aware that their lives will never be the same.

And to my wife, Gayle.

Chapter One

The bright red Concord stage bounced around the sharp curve on the narrow, rocky road that opened onto the last stretch of the run from Point of Rocks to Tucson. Overhead, the bright October sun beamed down from a brittle blue sky upon the ribbon of dust boiling up behind the speeding stage.

A whip cracked, sounding like a gunshot above the clatter of hooves and the jangling of rigging. "Haiyee, Ben! Go, Joe," the jehu shouted, popping the rawhide whip above the heads of the close-hitched team. The Concord hit another curve, and the driver skillfully slid the two thousand pound coach around it.

Clint Bowles, the jehu, rocked in rhythm with the bouncing stage, three pairs of reins laced between the fingers of his left hand and his right gripping the hickory stock of his braided-rawhide whip as he played the ribbons with a sensitive touch. His gray eyes swept the road ahead, quartering to the jumble of boulders off to the north and the saguaro–dotted desert to the south.

Speck Adams, his partner, rode shotgun, his freckled face contorted in frustration. "Blast it, Clint. You can't go back. You been gone now over ten years. Everyone's done figured you dead and dried up. Go back now, and you'll be back on the dodge from the law. Now, I don't know what all took place back then. It ain't none of my business. Why, you ain't even sure this jasper is the same Sam Cooper. You said yourself he was dead."

Keeping his eyes fixed on the rock-strewn road ahead, Clint grunted. Ever since two days ago when the drummer told him about the old man fighting to keep his ranch up around Santa Fe, he'd done nothing but consider the same arguments Speck was throwing at him.

At first, Clint had dismissed the story. The Sam Cooper he had known had been dead ten years. Besides, he didn't have a ranch, only a livery in the pueblo of El Jardin, New Mexico Territory.

But, the one argument that gave substance to the story was the missing two fingers on Cooper's left hand. Clint was the reason old Sam had lost them. Cooper's fingers had been hacked off by a Comanche tomahawk when he was rescuing Clint from the savages. "You're probably right, but I got to see for myself."

Speck snorted. "So you go and see. What happens if someone finds out that Cleve Bollinger didn't burn up at that fire in Valverde?"

"Bollinger was years ago," Clint muttered.

"Maybe so, but folks got memories, especially about gunfighters, and no one who was around that part of the territory at the time is going to forget the likes of Cleve Bollinger." He paused, then added. "A man's got just so much luck, partner. You used most of yours up when that poor jasper got his-self burned up, and they found him wearing your ivory-handled six-shooter."

A rabbit darted across the narrow road directly in front of the team. The near leader shied, but Clint steadied him gently with a slight tug of his finger on the ribbons. He drew a deep breath, suddenly aware that the sense of well-being he had managed to achieve over the last few years was beginning to crumble.

Speck was right. Clint had somehow always managed to come up with more than his share of luck. He fingered the deep scar on his cheek, one so deep that not even the wiry whiskers covering his broad jaw would grow through it. "I can't argue with you, Speck. I've been given a heap of luck, but now I got me a chance to make right a terrible wrong if I can. I didn't know Sam was still alive. I figured I'd killed him."

Ahead, the stock-tender threw open the corral gate at the home station of Western Trail Freight Lines and led a fresh team out. A young helper stood by, ready to switch the teams out and send the stage on its way to the swing station at San Pedro, thirteen miles to the west.

Clint deftly brought the exhausted team to a halt. He set the brake with the heel of his boot, tossed the reins to the stock-tender, and clambered to the ground.

Speck looked down at his partner. With a trace of disgust in his voice, he growled, "You listen to anything I said?"

Clint grinned up at him. "Every word."

With a snort, Speck shook his head. "At least don't make up your mind until you sleep on it tonight, you hear?"

For a moment, Clint hesitated, then nodded. "All right. I'll sleep on it. Come morning, I'll let you know."

Speck started to climb down. "I pure-dee hope so. Now, let's get inside and let old Case know we're back."

Clint gave his partner's back a crooked grin. "Case? Who do you think you're fooling? You just want to get in there and make sweet eyes at Case's pretty little niece."

Speck glanced over his shoulder, his freckle face flaming red. He snapped back gruffly. "That ain't so, and besides, what of it?" He turned to face Clint.

With a warm laugh, Clint slapped him on a thin shoulder. "Not a thing, partner. Not a blasted thing. You just go right ahead and make fish-goggle eyes at that pretty little thing."

A few hundred miles to the northeast, *el Alcalde,* John Rawlings, his feet set wide apart, stood proudly on the balcony of his lavish *hacienda,* looking out over the *bosques* and meadows of the Sangre de Cristo Mountains stretching to the south and east as far as the eye could see. He pulled a fat, black cigar from his vest pocket and bit off the tip. Touching a lucifer to it, he gazed with smug satisfaction over his empire, which now, after the federal government's treaty with the Navaho at Bosque Redondo the past June, would triple in size.

The meadows burgeoned with lush grass, and the mountain slopes bulged with minerals. And in less than a year, the Atchison, Topeka, and Santa Fe Railroad would be clamoring for a right of way across the land before him.

Soon he would own it all, and with land came power, the power derived from lucrative federal appointments that would be given him by the office of the president of the United States, Andrew Johnson, thanks to the influence of the Secretary of State, William H. Seward.

For the last five years, he had schemed his way through the political labyrinths of territorial power and put together a network of influence no one could overcome.

As a result of the old Spanish land grants, land titles were cloudy, and ownership was difficult to prove. In fact, the only title most landowners could claim was possession, so Rawlings had hired the most able attorneys at generous wages to pursue the web of title searches that had eventually evicted the majority of the squatters.

The evictions created another problem. The small landowners vowed to fight him to their last breath, but he managed to come up with the last pieces of the puzzle that would guarantee him the power he sought, Sheriff Hitch Faber and Judge J.B. Hyde.

With Hyde on the bench, the small landowners would be going against the law, which was efficiently run by Sheriff Faber. That was all Rawlings needed.

He threw out his chest in satisfaction and blew a thick stream of cigar smoke into the air.

The glaring sunlight flashed on the gleaming blade of the razor-edged sword as it sliced in a downward arc at the Confederate soldier sprawled in the red Georgia mud.

His Spenser rifle clutched in his knotted fists, Corporal Clint Bowles grunted between clenched teeth and frantically extended his arms, blocking the downward blow of the deadly blade.

Sparks flew as the blade slammed into the blue metal of the barrel and skidded into the hammer. With a frantic growl, Bowles rolled to his left and slammed the butt of the Spenser into the Yankee lieutenant's shoulder, sending him tumbling into a ditch filled with mud made slick with both northern and southern blood, but not before the tip of the blade laid open the corporal's cheek like a hog at butchering time.

Chapter Two

Abruptly, Clint jerked awake, sitting upright on his bunk of rough-hewn timbers and taut ropes, his breath coming in sharp gasps. He shook his head and dug knotted fists into the sweat stinging his eyes. He blinked several times in an effort to focus on the pale moonlight that poured a wide swath through the window.

For several moments, he sat motionless, his bearded chin resting on his chest, his breathing slowing. It had been almost two years since the dream had haunted him, but now, with the revelation that Sam Cooper might still be alive, his past came rushing back, the memories tearing open old wounds, threatening to destroy the life he had managed to build, and ripping open the one he had hoped to hide.

He stared out the window into the pale moonlight lighting the Arizona desert. Thoughtfully, he ran the callused tip of his finger over the thick scar on his cheek.

In the dark night beyond the adobe came the familiar chirruping of crickets, the hoot of owls, and the skree of hawks resonating through the cool air.

Far in the distance, somewhere out in the angular shadows cast by the giant saguaros, the plaintive squeal of a rabbit punctuated the night with a chilling cry.

He glanced into the darkness enveloping the far side of the room where his partner snored softly. He muttered under his breath. "Why now? Just when all my plans are coming together, why now?"

Still, throughout all these years, despite hoping against hope, deep down he had known with a chilling certainty this day would come.

He fumbled in his shirt at the foot of his bunk for his bag of Bull Durham. Pausing before he rolled a smoke, he tugged on his boots as a guard against rattlesnakes and silently slipped from the small adobe he called home.

Outside, he touched a lucifer to his cigarette and inhaled deeply on the raw tobacco while he gazed up at the white band of the Milky Way spanning the dark heavens. The night was silent, save for faint laughter drifting across the desert from the Red Dog Saloon on the outskirts of Tucson.

From the position of the Big Dipper in the starry heavens, he knew it was almost two A.M.

For the last two days, ever since the drummer on the stage told him of the trouble up in New Mexico Territory, he had been fighting with himself, trying to find reasons not to throw away all he had managed to build since before the war simply because an old man he had thought dead for the last ten years might now be alive, and in trouble.

But even as Clint Bowles squatted outside his adobe, watching the sinuous shadow of a rattlesnake slithering through the bear grass and ocotillo, he knew he had to go to Santa Fe.

He shook his head wearily, trying not to think about the repercussions of his decision.

When Clint rose before sun-up next morning, Speck had the coffee boiling on the edge of the coals in the adobe fireplace. The lanky cowpoke grinned crookedly at Clint. "Sleeping late, huh?"

Sitting up on the edge of his bunk, Clint arched an eyebrow and scratched his jaw. "Coffee ready?"

"Yep." Speck poured a cup and plopped it down on the rough-hewn table. He rolled a cigarette. Without looking at Clint, he muttered. "So you made up your mind, huh?"

Clint eyed the lanky cowpoke suspiciously. "You were awake last night?"

"Couldn't help it. You made enough racket to wake the dead."

A crooked grin slid over Clint's rugged face. He shrugged and stepped into his trousers, tucked his shirt in the waist and buckled on his gunbelt.

Speck grew serious, the freckles on his face seeming to stand out like a bad case of chickenpox. "You reckon on what you're throwing away if you go up there? Five years honorable service in the Confederate army, three years of hard work since, the chance of a station manager's job over at Fort Yuma, and worst of all, maybe even a gunfighter's reputation coming back to haunt you."

After pouring a cup of steaming coffee, Clint sat across the battered table from his partner and studied him intently. "Got no choice, Speck. If that jasper is Sam Cooper, then I owe him. I thought I had got him killed up at Fort Selden. I saw him in his coffin before they buried him."

Speck held up his hand. "I know the story, and I know how you feel." He sipped his coffee and rolled a cigarette, he continued. "If it wasn't for the gunfighter reputation you was trying to hide, I'd say, go help the old man—if he is the same jasper. But if word gets out that you was Bollinger, the gunfighter who was faster than a snake, all you'll be doing the rest of your life is running. You really think Case Henry is going to give you a job in Yuma if he finds out you was Bollinger?" The freckle–faced cowpoke snorted. "Ain't no way. None at all."

For several seconds, Clint studied the black coffee steaming in the mug he cupped in his calloused hands. "I got no choice, Speck. That's it pure and simple."

Speck studied Clint in dismay. Outside an owl hooted. The lean cowpoke's face stiffened. Moments later, the owl hooted again, and then once again. Speck's eyes narrowed. "Hear that, Clint. I got a bad feeling about this. Mighty bad."

After eight years with Speck, Clint was well aware of his partner's obsession with superstitions. "Because of some old hooty owl?" He took one last drag on his cigarette and ground it under his boot heel. "I've told you a thousand times, Speck. Those superstitions of yours hold no more water than an Arbuckle's coffee sack."

Ignoring his partner's admonition, Speck shook his head. "No, Siree. I've seen it before. It's bad luck when a hooty owl hoots three times. Bad luck."

Well before the sun rose over the Catalina Mountains to the east, Clint and Speck reined up in front of the Western Trail Freight office and dismounted.

A sun-dried, bandy-legged old man waddled out from the corral and reached for the reins. "Morning, boys," he cackled. "Early, ain't you?"

"Reckon so, Dusty." Speck glanced up at the clear sky as he dismounted his yellow dun. "Looks to be a right pleasant day. Red sky last night."

With a weary sigh at the young man's superstitious announcement, Dusty rolled his phlegmy eyes and led the yellow dun and Clint's gray into the corral.

Ignoring the old man's skeptical grunt, Speck studied Clint. "I wish you'd think long and hard on this, partner."

Clint chuckled. "I have. Look, you don't have to ride along with me. Stay here and hold things down." He nodded to the office. "Besides, what about Miss Amy? After all, you're uglier than sin. Why, she might find herself some good-looking galoot while you're gone.

When I finish up there, I'll be back. Couldn't take more than a month or so."

The freckle-faced cowpoke glanced at the office. "Like you say, it won't take more than a month or so. And I ain't took care of you the last eight years just so you can go off and Lord only knows what'll happen to you. You know better than that."

Clint studied his *compadre* for several seconds. A faint grin played over his thin lips. "Obliged."

Case Henry, owner of Western Trail Freight, looked around from the pot bellied stove where he was pouring himself a cup of coffee when the two lanky cowpokes entered the office. He grimaced as a pain shot through his rotund belly. Too much mock apple pie the night before. "Morning, boys." He held up a tin cup. "Coffee's ready. Stage is due in fifteen minutes." He pointed the cup at the gray light of false dawn filling the window. "Should have an easy run to Soldiers' Farewell. Ain't heard much of no Apache trouble last few days, but the army is sending a patrol with the stage all the same."

Clint scratched his bearded jaw. "Reckon I need to talk to you about that, Case." He poured a cup of thick, black coffee. "This is my last run for a spell." He continued before his surprised boss could reply. "I got business up around Santa Fe." He sipped the coffee. "Important business. Figure it'll take about a month or so."

"That goes for me too, boss," Speck put in.

For several moments, Case studied the younger men. Neither had ever played him wrong. He shook his head.

"Santa Fe, huh?" He glanced at the empty desk where his niece, Amy Henry, kept the books for the company. "She'll miss you," he said to Speck.

The lanky cowpoke shrugged and ducked his head. "Like Clint said, Boss. It'll only be for a month or so."

The older man pursed his lips. "This is the middle of October. I reckon you boys could run into some rugged weather up there."

Clint chuckled. "Reckon so. We'll have to face it when it happens."

The freight owner sighed. With typical western resignation, he replied. "If your mind's made up."

"It is."

"Well, Joe Hampton and Fred Carson are the relief drivers at Soldiers' Farewell. Tell them to bring the stage back in your place. Tie your ponies on the back of the stage. Save a trip back here."

Clint nodded.

Henry rubbed the heavy jowls on his aging face and studied Clint. "You coming back?" He nodded to Speck. "I know this no-account is," he said with a chuckle. "Amy wouldn't have it any other way."

Speck grinned, a blush covered his skinny neck and face. A wry grin curled Clint's bearded face. "I dad-blamed well reckon on it." In his mind, he added, *if I'm lucky*.

"Good." Henry nodded. "Get back in time, and that job in Yuma is still yours. You hear? With you there and Speck here, and my brains, boys, we can build us a blasted empire."

With a wistful look at the empty desk, Speck cleared his throat. "I'd be obliged if you tell Miss Amy goodbye for me, Boss."

Henry nodded briefly, then turned to Clint. "Don't suppose you'd tell me what's going on?"

Downing the rest of his coffee, Clint lifted an eyebrow. "Nope."

Case watched as the stage pulled out. He had a sick feeling in his stomach he'd never see those two boys again.

Chapter Three

Late that afternoon, the rocking stage topped the crest of a gentle slope and swept around a sharp curve, swaying on its oxhide thoroughbraces. "There she be," muttered Speck, pointing the muzzle of his Spenser at the way-station in the valley below.

The home station at Soldiers' Farewell was typical of most western stations in dry country, constructed of adobe bricks and topped by a solid flat roof supported by thick beams, the ends of which protruded from the thick walls of the station several feet, allowing for a slatted porch that offered a shady respite from the blistering sun.

Popping the leather ribbons gently with his left hand, Clint nodded and glanced at the lengthening shadows the setting sun cast on the rocky desert around them. "After Joe and Fred take over the reins, I reckon we can

15

put another dozen miles behind us before dark," he muttered, nodding to the winding road ahead that cut northeast to Cook's Springs.

Speck rolled his eyes. "Why not spend the night here and get us a early start come morning?"

Keeping his gray eyes on the road ahead, Clint shrugged. "Sooner we get up there, the sooner we get back," he replied laconically, instinctively realizing that the harder he rode, the longer he stayed in the saddle, the less time his brain would be free to fester over what he was doing, and what he was giving up.

Speck muttered a curse. "Well, at least let's wait until I put myself around some grub. I've done had my Spanish dinner today," he muttered, referring to the cowboy habit of cinching up his belt another notch to dispel hunger. "I figure on a bait of sidemeat and beans."

The only bait of sidemeat and beans that Speck managed was a couple spoonfuls of *frijoles* and fatback dolloped between two thick chunks of sourdough bread before he swung into his saddle and hurried to catch up with Clint who had urged his gray into a running two-step heading for Cook's Springs, a solid day's ride to the northeast.

Behind them, the billowing dust kicked up by their ponies hung motionless in the still air. "Best I recollect," shouted Clint as Speck pulled up beside him. "Best I recollect, there's a *parajes* and waterhole in the hills just before we reach Cow Wallow."

"Cow Wallow?" Speck sputtered. "That's fifteen miles from here, and it's almost dark."

"Well, then," Clint chuckled, kicking his gray into a mile-eating trot. "We best waste no time."

Muttering a curse, Speck dug his spurs into his dun's flanks. "Reckon not," he growled, pushing his pony up beside Clint's gray. As he slipped into the rhythm of his dun's gait, he couldn't help thinking of Amy. A faint grin curled his thin lips. "You figure she was mad at me?" He called out above the thudding of hooves.

"What's that?" Clint shouted back.

"Amy. You think she's mad at me for running off?"

Cutting his eyes toward his partner, Clint grinned. "Naw. She understands. She's a fine lady. Too blasted good for the likes of you."

Speck grinned at him. "She is that."

An hour later, a waning moon rose over the jagged peaks of the Pinaleno Mountains to the east. "Cow Wallow is in the north foothills of the mountains yonder," Clint said. "Another hour or so, you can rest your bones."

The night grew colder, bringing with it a chill that made Clint wish for a cup of steaming coffee, but he knew he had to forego the coffee tonight, they were making cold *parajes*, wary of any passing Kiowa or Apache.

As Clint rolled out his soogan, Speck muttered. "What about your rope?"

"Rope?"

"You heard me," the lanky cowboy replied, laying out his rawhide rope in a circle around his soogan. "Unless you want a rattler as a bed partner tonight."

Clint snorted. "I reckon I'll chance it," he replied, slipping between his blankets and pulling the tarp up to his neck.

"Have it your own way," Speck shot back. "Just don't go asking me to suck out no poison, you hear?"

"I hear, Mama."

A few moments later, Speck heard Clint chuckle. "What's wrong with you?" He muttered.

"Nothing. I was just imagining how Miss Amy was going to have her hands full straightening you out about all that superstition nonsense."

Speck grunted and jerked the tarp up over his head.

Speck awakened next morning to a blazing fire and the smell of boiling coffee. He blinked once or twice and spotted Clint squatting in front of the fire, tending slabs of meat on spits by the fire.

Clint glanced around, grinning at the frown on his partner's face. "About time you woke up. You missed our guests."

"Guests?" Speck propped himself up on one elbow. "What guests?"

Pointing the blade of his knife at the broiling meat, Clint replied. "*Pindah-lickolee.*"

Speck frowned. "Pinda–Who the Sam Hill you talking about?"

Shaking his head, the rawhide–tough cowpoke sliced a chunk of broiling meat from the slab and replied. "*Ojo Blanco*, the old Apache. White Eye. Remember him?"

A sheepish grin split the lanky cowboy's slender face.

"White Eye. You bet, I remember him. The one you cut the bullet out of." He glanced around the small camp. "He was here?"

"Two hours ago. Spotted us back at Apache Pass and followed. A heap of young Mescalero Apache bucks is out raiding. He wanted to make certain they didn't mess with us."

With an infectious grin, Speck rolled out of his soogan, eyeing the thin slices of venison popping and sizzling over the fire. "Next time we see the old man, remind me to thank him."

Clint grinned. Speck might have the chance sooner than he expected despite the old warrior's claim he was heading for the Sierra Madres down in Mexico to winter, Clint figured *Ojo Blanco* and his handful of warriors would be tagging after the two of them all the way to Santa Fe.

Though the day dawned hot and dry, just before noon heavy clouds, bellies dark with snow, blew in, and a chill wind curled around the mountain peaks of the Gila Mountains.

Speck turned his shoulder into the biting winds. "Hole up or what?"

Clint glanced up at the doughnut shaped clouds curling around the granite peaks of the towering mountains. Below them lay ten miles of alkali flats. "Cook's Springs is an hour, maybe two east of us," he muttered, pulling out his wool Mackinaw and buttoning it up against the razor edges of the icy gale blasting down from the Gilas. "We'll hole up there for the night with old Jess and his family."

The storm struck before they were half way across the alkali flats, the first edges slashed across the white flats with the cut of a skinning knife.

Clint leaned over his gray's neck and dug his spurs into the animal's flanks. "Let's get while we can. Won't be long before we can see nothing but snow."

Speck spurred his yellow dun up beside the gray, and for the next twenty minutes, the two animals pounded across the rock-hard flats.

"Lordy lord," Speck muttered, leaning over his pony's neck and cocking his head to gaze in disbelief beyond Clint. "Look at that, would you? I told you that hooty owl meant bad luck." The swirling wind whipped his words from his lips.

Clint shot a look back to the north. The sight froze his blood.

A white wall of snow hurtled across the flats toward them. And he knew when it hit, the blinding blizzard would obliterate everything around them, swallowing them up in a howling vortex of white like a tornado.

Clenching his teeth, the rawhide–tough cowpoke laid the leather to his pony, and the frightened animal responded with a powerful stride that ate up the miles. "Stay close," he shouted to Speck above the howl of the storm.

The blizzard plowed into them, almost knocking their horses off stride. The two desperate cowboys struggled to hold their ponies in check, pulling them back down into a trot, then a walk.

"Blast it, Clint. I can't see nothing," Speck shouted, from time to time, his yellow dun bouncing against Clint's gray.

Clint cut his eyes to the right, but all he could make out was a fuzzy figure engulfed in swirling white flakes. Despite the howling of the vicious storm, he could hear the labored grunts of their horses.

Having covered this trail dozens of times on the stage over the last three years, he was familiar with various landmarks, but the storm had obliterated them.

Time dragged. The storm roared in his ears. Through the wailing of the blizzard, he heard Speck's frantic voice. "We got to hole up somewhere, Clint. We're running blind."

Clint grimaced. Speck was right. Either they pulled up now, or they could end up fifty miles from any source of help. But where? The alkali flats was no place to weather out a blizzard.

Suddenly, he felt his gray stiffen under his legs. The pony whinnied. Clint squinted into the driving snow and saw his horse's ears perked forward. Moments later, the welcome smell of woodsmoke stung his nostrils.

"Clint!" Speck shouted. "We made it. We made it."

Without warning, the low silhouette of Cook's Springs station loomed ahead. Clint's gray whinnied again, and moments later, a dim light appeared in the storm. A voice shouted, "Hello! Someone out there?"

"Jess! Over here," Clint shouted back.

The lantern surged forward and a hand reached up for the bridle. A bearded man looked up in surprise. Behind him stood a young boy, no older than sixteen. "Why, bless my soul," the stock-tender exclaimed. "Clint Bowles." A broad grin came to his rugged face. "Get in here where it's warm, boys. My woman's got hot stew. The boy and me'll put up your ponies. Looks like this little blow might last a spell."

Chapter Four

Clint and Speck stomped inside, beating on their arms in an effort to drive some heat back into their almost frozen bones. The dancing flames in the fireplace drew them like moths.

Across the room, three grizzled hardcases sat hunched over a table, sharing an almost empty bottle of whiskey. Clint nodded and made his way to the fire, holding out his hands and soaking up the welcome heat.

A curtain, behind which Jess maintained his family quarters, separated the rectangular room. Moments later, a slender Navaho woman wearing a flowing skirt and a wool jacket buttoned up around her neck emerged from behind the curtain followed by a young Indian maiden carrying a stack of tin plates.

Clint nodded. "Howdy, Miz Swink. Cornflower."

With a faint smile, the older woman acknowledged Clint's greeting and went about busying herself in front of a freestanding adobe fireplace in which a pot of stew bubbled. Cornflower smiled shyly and quickly set the tin plates on the table. Without a glance to either side, she hurried back behind the curtain.

Across the room, one of the hardcases arched a lascivious eyebrow at his partners. A sneer played over their lips.

Abruptly, the door swung open. Jess Swink and his young son, Lamy, scurried in followed by a burst of snow that spread across the room. "Brrr," Jess shouted. "It's colder than—" He hesitated a moment, giving his wife a sheepish grin. "Than the dickens," he added, grinning at Clink and Speck.

His wife went back to tending her stew, a faint smile on her lips.

One of the hardcases called out. "Hey, boy. Have that sister of yours bring us another bottle. And be quick about it."

Young Lamy looked up at his pa, a questioning frown on his forehead. Jess' face darkened, and he jerked his head in the direction of the curtain. "I'll take care of it, boy. You get in the back."

The grizzled cowpoke shook his head. "Not you, old man. That half-breed daughter of yours. Ain't that right, Al?"

"Yeah," laughed Al, a smaller cut of the loud-mouthed hardcase. "She's a heap more fetching than you, old man."

The third hardcase grimaced. He shook his head. "Forget it, Pete. A squaw ain't worth causing no trouble."

Pete shook the third man's hand off. "Stay out of this, Joe. You're too young to know what's choice and what ain't."

Jess ignored them, going behind the bar and reaching for a bottle of whiskey. "I'll get it for you, Pete," he announced.

Pete shoved his chair back and swayed to his feet, his eyes cold as the raging storm outside. His hand resting on the butt of his sixgun. He growled. "I said fetch out that good-looking, half-breed squaw you got back there. I want her to bring me the bottle. You hear me, old man?"

A cold voice from the other end of the room cut through the tension. "You got such a big mouth, it's hard not to hear you, Mister."

Cutting his pig eyes in the direction of the voice, Pete Bodine glared at the bearded cowpoke standing in front of the fire. A chill ran up his spine. The cowpoke's arms hung limp at his side, the fingers of each hand inches from the hoglegs tied down on his slender hips. A bitter twist curled his lips, and for a fleeting moment, Pete thought he spotted a gleam of eagerness in the jasper's eyes.

"This ain't none of your business, cowboy," he hissed, noting the scar running across the jasper's cheek.

In a flat voice, Clint replied. "I'm making it my business."

Pete gulped, suddenly wary of the stranger. No one had ever questioned his massive body or his grotesque snarl. He glanced down at his brothers, but their eyes were on the cowpoke at the other end of the room. "Don't do nothing you'll regret, cowboy," he managed to croak out.

Clint sensed the long unfamiliar surge of anger mixed with excitement welling up inside, the adrenaline gunfighters savored. A distant roar filled his ears, and his blood ran hot. "You're all talk, Pete. Either sit down and keep your mouth shut or slap leather."

The grizzled hardcase dragged the tip of his tongue across his lips. He glanced nervously at his brothers. "You're forgetting. There's three of us."

"And there's three of us," Jess said off to one side, lifting the muzzle of a Henry and lining it up on Pete's chest. Beside him, his son did the same.

"Make that four," drawled Speck, his Colt appearing in his hand.

Bodine glared murderously at Clint, the air crackling with electricity. His shoulders hunched forward, he flexed his fingers, his whole body balanced precipitously on the razor's edge of impulse. Finally, with a sigh, he held his hands out to the side and shook his head. "It ain't worth it." He plopped back down in his chair, but the rage in his wild eyes spoke volumes, sending a message Clint understood. "We'll meet again, cowboy," he growled. Without taking his burning eyes off Clint, he muttered to Jess. "Just bring us a bottle, barkeep."

"That'll be a dollar," Jess said, setting the whiskey on the table, but keeping his fingers about the neck of the bottle.

The other brother, Al, glared up at him angrily, but the youngest of the bunch simply chuckled and tossed a coin on the table. "Obliged," young Joe muttered, his cold voice belying the smile on his face.

Pete said nothing. He just kept his black eyes on the bottle of whiskey.

Clint watched the big man warily, sensing a smoldering flame that could explode into a raging inferno at any moment.

Later that night, their bellies filled with a sumptuous supper of hot venison stew, Clint and Speck sat in front of the fire sipping whiskey-laced coffee and enjoying a smoke. Clint had judiciously placed his straight back chair so he could keep a wary eye on the three jaspers at the far end of the room who had climbed into their bedrolls.

Jess pulled a chair up to the fire and poured a shot of whiskey. He glanced at the three brothers snoring noisily. "Them are the Bodine brothers. Mighty glad they's gone to sleep. That oldest one, Pete, the one doing all the yapping—he' sort of tetched in the head. Crazy-tetched like. Near kilt a man with his hands over in Yuma."

Clint nodded. He'd heard the story.

Jess continued. "Trouble tags after them like dirt on a bullwhacker's boots. Glad when they light a shuck out of here."

For two interminable days, the raging blizzard swept through the jagged mountains and across the dried up *lagunas* and the rock-filled basins through which the wagon route meandered.

Though no further words of anger or recrimination were spoken between the two parties, a seething undercurrent of rage permeated the closed quarters; the air boiled with tension; however, the three hardcases remained silent, going out of their way to displease no one, but Pete's glittering black eyes tracked every step Clint took.

The middle Bodine, Al, kept a wary eye on his older brother. As long as he could remember, there were times when Pete went crazy wild. Before their pa was hung for horse stealing, the old man had once opined that something in his oldest son's brain had never connected. Al rolled his eyes. He hoped this wasn't going to be one of them times.

The third morning dawned bright and clear, lighting the snow-covered countryside in a dazzling array of glittering diamonds.

Within an hour, the three Bodines swung into the saddle. Without a word, Pete glared at Clint. The big man's black eyes blazed. The muscles in his jaws twitched like a tangle of snakes. "I ain't forgetting you, cowboy," he growled.

A taunting smile creased the heavy beard covering Clint's face. "If you was smart, you would, but from what I've seen, Pete, that particular quality ain't one of your strong suits."

Pete's eyes blazed. He yanked his pony around and

dug his spurs into the startled horse's flanks, sending the animal racing east along Cook's Wagon Route toward Santa Fe.

Speck grunted. "Kinda adding coal oil to the fire, ain't you, partner?"

Clint arched an eyebrow. "To blazes with him."

Chapter Five

Jess came to stand beside Clint and Speck on the porch. "You boys best watch out for them, Pete especially."

Studying the three hardcases as they slowly disappeared into the glistening snow to the east along the route Speck and Clint had planned to take, Clint muttered, "I reckon since those old boys are heading that-a-way, we'd be smart to cut down south to the Peloncillos, come out around Dona Ana."

Speck chuckled. "I ain't going to argue with you on that, partner."

An hour out of Cook's Springs where the trail swerved to the south and dipped through a small stream under a canopy of stunted oaks that prevented snow from reaching the ground, Pete angled upstream around a jumble of boulders overlooking the trail. "The youngest of the Bodine brothers, Joe, frowned. "Where are you going, Pete? It's too early to find a camp for the night."

"Shut up and follow me," the grizzled hardcase growled. "I'm going to give that cowboy what I promised him."

Joe grimaced at Al who rolled his eyes and shook his head in frustration. More than once, he had seen Pete get caught up in some crazy situation, so crazy that the older brother could think of nothing else until he had gotten his satisfaction.

And more than once, trying to calm his brother, Al had suffered a beating until he learned his lesson and said nothing.

Clint and Speck pulled out of the way-station, heading southeast, skirting the northern foothills of the rugged Peloncillo Mountains several miles south of the ambush set up by Pete before cutting back under Cook's Peak and aiming for Fort Cummings and then, a few miles farther on, San Diego on the banks of the Rio Grande.

At San Diego, they put up for the night in a small inn with three other guests, one a Mexican *ranchero* from Dona Ana, a small village to the south on the east bank of the muddy river.

The young *ranchero*, Don Hidalgo de Ornate, accompanied by two of his trusted *vaqueros*, was journeying to a *rancho* west of Fort Craig to buy cattle for his own *rancho* south of Dona Ana.

The small party of new friends spent a pleasant evening enjoying the warmth of a small fire from the adobe fireplace and sampling vintage wine Don Hidalgo had brought from his own vineyards.

Upon Clint's suggestion that Don Hidalgo could save two or three days travel by taking the east bank of the river, the young aristocrat explained. "*Si*, but there, *amigo,* one must face *jornado del muerto,* the journey of death." He shrugged. "I will gladly expend three days rather than tempt the gods in such a *despoblado,* a place of desolation."

Banding together, they trailed to the north following Cook's Wagon Route along the western shore of the Rio Grande, passing through the pueblo of Santa Barbara, then Fort McRae, and on up to Fort Craig across the river from *Paraje de Fray cristobal*.

While five well-armed riders would present an imposing force against any random attacks from small war parties, Clint remained alert, his eyes constantly quartering the country around them. The three Bodines remained in the back of his head.

That night, after the fire had burned down, Speck whispered from his soogan, "Reckon you know where we are, huh?"

"Been on my mind all day," Clint mumbled. "Ever since we passed the road to Fray Cristobal."

Neither spoke any further, but each was remembering the inferno eight years earlier that consumed the cantina in the small village of Valverde, north of Fray Cristobal, leaving only blackened ruins and, as far as the territorial law was concerned, the charred body of the gunfighter, Cleve Bollinger.

Next morning, Don Hidalgo reined up at a fork in the road. "Here is where we must part, my friends." He gestured up the winding road that twisted up into the Gallinas Mountains. "My destination is the *rancho* of Jesus Bernalillo."

Clint nodded. "You take care."

"And you my friend. Should you come to Dona Ana, ask for me. All in the village know my *rancho.*"

As the young aristocrat and his *vaqueros* rode away, Speck drawled, "That Don Hidalgo seems to be a right hospitable jasper."

Clint nodded. "Yep. The kind to ride the river with."

While the weather had moderated the last few days, Clint knew from experience that the warmer weather was merely a portent of the biting cold to come. From experience, he guessed they had only a few days before the next blizzard struck, and since they were moving into higher country, the intensity of the storm would be even more threatening.

Speck rested his hands on the saddle horn and leaned forward. He gestured to the foothills of the Gallinas Mountains, which were covered with the glorious yellow of cottonwoods awaiting the chilling winds of winter. "Ain't this a sight to behold, partner? Look at that valley yonder. Why that grass looks so good that I reckon we could raise us a two year old heifer in just six months."

Clint shook his head and grinned. "You reckon so, huh?" He had to admit, the soil in the meadows was rich, and the grass luxuriant. Once he had dreamed of such a *rancho*, but fate, and a foolish decision had sent his life careening in another direction.

From the corner of his eye, he saw Speck gazing out over the magnificent panorama before them. With Amy, Speck would have the chance to build such a *rancho*. But he himself didn't figure that opportunity would ever come his way.

A breeze from the river brought with it the smell of wet sand, and from time to time the strident shrieks of sandhill cranes broke the rhythmic squeak of leather and the grunt of their ponies trudging along the rocky road. Across the river to the east, the barren slopes of the Fray Cristobal Mountains rose against a blood red sun, and to the southeast stretched the long blue serrations of the San Andres Mountains.

From time to time, Clint spotted dark figures on the jagged peaks, but he said nothing. He hoped they were Ojo Blanco's warriors looking over them and not a renegade band of Kiowa or Apaches raiding along the river.

As they climbed higher and higher, the air grew thinner, and the adobe dwellings gave way to rugged structures of stone or logs, materials better suited for the winters that pounded the mountain peaks.

"Where to you reckon we are now?" Speck asked,

glancing at the jagged range of mountains piercing the cloudless blue sky far to his left. To his right, the Rio Grande bubbled and churned southward in a shallow bed.

Clint studied the country around him. "If I remember right, a few miles ahead is Casa Colorado. Albuquerque is only a couple days beyond."

Speck shivered. "I don't know about you, partner, but I sure cotton for a nice warm fire tonight. My toes is just about froze off."

Clint chuckled. He gestured to the foothills covered with yucca and sotol, interspersed with prickly pear and creosote bushes. "You got no argument from me about that. In all these foothills, we're bound to find a cozy *paraje* for the night. And," he added, noting the abundance of creosote bushes. "From the looks, we got us a heap of firewood if you don't mind the smell."

Speck grinned crookedly. "As long as I'm warm."

The two cowpokes rode across a snug camp in the middle of several granite upthrusts surrounding a small pool of sweet spring water with a thin skim of ice covering its surface.

Clint reined up. "This is just about as good as we'll find. What do you think?"

Speck looked at him in surprise, then nodded to the blue sky overhead. "You sure you're feeling all right, Clint? There's still an hour of daylight left. We can make another few miles."

Clint arched an eyebrow.

Speck hastened to add, "Now, don't misunderstand me. I'm all for taking a few extra hours to rest up. The bones in my lanky behind are wearing holes in my saddle."

The cowboy glanced up at the peak where the dark figures had been. He grinned. "Truth is, old friend. I wouldn't mind a few hours of rest too. We been pushing mighty hard the last few days. Hot coffee and a full belly will do us both good. Besides I reckon we'll be reaching Albuquerque soon enough."

Speck snorted. "You ain't getting no argument from me."

The clatter of hooves interrupted him. The lanky cowpoke grabbed for his sixgun, but Clint stayed him. "Easy, there, Speck. Easy. We got company coming, that's all."

Speck frowned. "Company? Who the—"

At that moment, Ojo Blanco and two warriors rode in to the *paraje* with a young doe strung over the rump of one of their pintos.

After dropping off the doe, one of the young warriors disappeared back into the night while the other deftly strung up the animal and sliced steaks from a hindquarter. "Strong Swimmer watch from below," Ojo Blanco announced. "No trouble."

Around the fire later that night, the old Apache warrior nodded to the west. "Three white men look for you, but you not come."

Clint and Speck exchanged knowing glances. "On the wagon route out of Cook's Springs?"

Ojo Blanco nodded and ripped off a chunk of venison with his gleaming white teeth. "*Si*. They wait two days, then ride on to Fort McRae."

Speck eyed Clint a moment, then turned to Ojo Blanco. "Whereabouts are them old boys now?"

Rubbing his greasy fingers through his long black hair, Ojo Blanco spoke rapidly to the young warrior at his side. Though Clint had spent time with the Apache, the words were lost on him.

The young brave gestured to the south. Ojo Blanco nodded. "Hair Rope, he say the white men stay at fort, three days from here." He shrugged. "But, who can say?"

Clint nodded to Hair Rope, a young, broad-chested Apache warrior. He touched his thumb to the tips of his fingers and laid them over his heart, and then made a slashing motion forward and touched his forehead, signifying that Hair Rope was a wise and clever man with a good heart.

A faint smile flickered over the young warrior's lips momentarily, then vanished, but the gleam of satisfaction in the young man's eyes told Clint his compliment had been well taken.

Speck tore off a bit of venison. "You reckon they'll be coming up this way, Clint?" He asked while chewing.

"Can't tell." Clint studied the coffee cup in his hands. "Jaspers like that sometimes get themselves all eaten up by hate, so much that it drives out all sense of reason. We might never see those jaspers again, or they could pop up right here in the middle of the night." He shook his head. "Can't tell about those kind." He glanced around at Ojo Blanco. "You ride with us to Santa Fe?"

The older warrior studied Clint a moment. He gestured to the road below. "You go. We—" He touched his greasy fingers to his chest and then indicated the forests and *bosques* covering the mountains. "We go there."

At that moment from the darkness beyond the *paraje,* a series of several pure notes, each rising to the crescendo of the thrush broke the silence. Ojo Blanco's eyes narrowed. Moments later, Strong Swimmer glided into the firelight. He nodded to the river. "Kiowa and Comanche. Make camp at *Lago del Muerto.*"

Clint frowned at Ojo. The old Apache explained. "Beyond the river high in the mountains is a lake of sweet water, sometimes full and sweet, sometimes dry. It is called the Lake of the Dead. Many warriors camp there tonight."

As he spoke, Strong Swimmer and Hair Rope extinguished the fire. "Go now. We ride with you to the Pueblo Lopez. It is but a few hours from here."

Chapter Six

As the sun rose over the northern foothills of the San Andres Mountains, Ojo Blanco reined up behind a tumble of jagged boulders on the crest of a rise overlooking Pueblo Lopez. "We leave you here," he announced.

Clint nodded, linking the forefingers of his hands in front of his chest, a sign that indicated friendship.

A faint smile played over Ojo Blanco's thin lips and he turned his gaze beyond the fort. "Journey with the spirits,' he said, touching the back of his hand to his forehead and extending his first and second fingers.

Clint grunted, "You too, old friend."

The two cowpokes reined up in front of the sutler's in the small village where they stocked up on corn meal, coffee, and bacon.

Less than twenty-four hours after Clint and Speck

disappeared behind a *bosque* of pine north of Pueblo Lopez, the Bodines rode into the small village from the south.

Pete pulled up at the first cantina. "Pick us up some grub at the sutler's," he muttered to his younger brother. "We'll be in the saloon. That bearded jasper and the freckle-faced kid might have come through here."

As the sun dropped behind the mountains far to the west, Clint and Speck spotted Socorro, the last pueblo on the western bank of the Rio Grande before reaching Pueblo Isleta, a few miles south of Albuquerque.

As every previous night, they found a secluded *paraje,* made an early fire, and then let it burn down before dark. They traveled warily, alert to their surroundings. More than once over the next few days, they pulled off the trail and watched as riders passed. Though none seemed threatening, Clint and Speck remained unseen back in the thick stands of aspen and pine and fir.

After the small pueblos of Isleta, Pajarito, and Atrisco, Albuquerque was a metropolis, its narrow *calles* filled with *carretas* and carts of various descriptions and condition.

Clint eyed the bustling community warily as they rode in, only a few eyes turned their way, quickly dismissing the white *gringos* as drifters.

Pulling in front of the Exchange Hotel, Clint and Speck eyed the establishment, noting several anglos entering and departing. Next door was a livery and beyond it a cantina.

"This place should do. Let's get a room, then take care of our ponies, and find someplace to wash the alkali out of our throats," Clint drawled, climbing down from his saddle.

Later that evening in the dining room, Clint and Speck put themselves around a thick steak, fried potatoes, and topped off with hot berry pie. Afterward, with their bellies stretched tighter than a Kiowa drumhead, they leaned back in their chairs and lit up a black cigar to enjoy with a last cup of steaming coffee.

That was when the local sheriff approached, a tall, rawboned anglo with an amiable grin on his face.

"Howdy, boys," he said, stopping at the table and peering down at them with cold eyes that belied the grin on his face. "I seen you was strangers. Thought I'd make sure the town was treating you right."

"Reckon so, Sheriff," Speck replied affably. "Right friendly town you got here." A tiny frown knit his brows when he noticed the sheriff had fastened a button in the wrong buttonhole.

Clint studied the angular man, knowing the sheriff was on a fishing trip, trying to find out the business of two strange anglos in town. He chuckled.

The sheriff frowned. "Something funny, cowboy?"

Clint held up his hand. "I meant nothing by it, Sheriff, but I've been around enough to know you didn't come in here just to make sure two strangers are being took care of properly." He sipped his coffee. "Let me put your mind to ease, Sheriff. We're here for one night. We already stocked up with grub from the Mexican place across the street. Come sun up, we'll be heading north to visit an old friend up to the northeast. So, why don't you have a seat and let me buy you a cup of coffee. You got so many streets in this town, I reckon we'll need help getting out."

For a moment, the sheriff studied Clint, then grinned and extended his hand. "Be right pleased for a cup. I'm Sheriff Aleman."

"I'm Clint Bowles, and this here is Speck Adams. We've come over from Tucson in Arizona Territory. Going up to visit an old friend at El Jardin."

The smile on the sheriff's face froze. He arched an eyebrow and plopped down in the chair. "El Jardin? You from around there?"

Speck shot Clint a puzzled look.

Clint shook his head and glibly lied. "Nope. Never been in this part of the country before. You know the place?"

The waiter slid the coffee on the table in front of the sheriff. "Heard about it," the sheriff replied, extracting a spoon from a pile of utensils on the table and dumping in a couple spoonfuls of sugar. "Never been up there, but from what I hear, it don't much cotton to outsiders. That's why I wondered if you was from thereabouts."

"Unfriendly town, huh?"

Sheriff Aleman shrugged. "From what I hear."

"Well, we're just going up to see a friend, reckon if we hit town, it'll only be to pass on through just like here."

"Yep," Speck chimed in. "We don't plan on no trouble. None at all."

Pouring some coffee in a saucer, the sheriff blew on it. "You boys seem right sensible, so I'll pass along what I hear. Just talk, you understand, but you hear enough, you figure there might be something to it. I don't know no names, but from stories over the last few years, El Jardin is run by jaspers who won't tolerate no one butting in. I reckon it has to do with the mining up there."

Clint feigned a frown. "Mining? Gold?"

He shrugged. "I don't know. Maybe silver and even copper. Jasper hears all sorts of talk. Far as I know, might even be the railroad."

Speck pondered the remark a moment. "What about the law? Don't it have some sayso?"

The sheriff grinned sheepishly. "Truth is, there ain't much law up there, if any. What with this being a territory, honest lawman are hard to find." He turned up the saucer and slurped the coffee down. "There be some of us who try to follow the law, but—we're few and far between."

That night, Clint lay staring at the dim cracks of light cast on the ceiling from the torchlights lining the *calle* below. Laughter from the cantina next to the livery and raucous shouts from the street drifted through the shuttered window.

Speck's voice came from the shadows on the far side of the room. "You awake?"

"Yeah."

"Clint, what the sheriff had to say make sense to you?"

"No. When I was there, it was just a regular little town. Nothing like what Aleman said. Of course, that was ten years ago."

"You think he was telling us the truth then?"

"Reckon so. What reason would he have to lie?"

Speck sighed heavily. "I don't know, but I ain't particularly looking forward to our visit now. I got a bad feeling." He paused. "I didn't say nothing about it, but when that sheriff picked up that spoon from that pile on the table, he crossed the fork over the knife, and everyone knows that's mighty bad luck. And to top that off, he'd buttoned a button in the wrong hole. That makes for double bad luck."

Clint groaned. "If you don't hush up about that bad luck nonsense, I'm going to bust every mirror I see. Then what'll you do?"

For several moments, Speck said nothing. Finally, in a resigned voice, he replied, "I reckon I wouldn't have no choice but to just find me a new partner."

Clint snorted. He rolled over and pulled the blankets up around his neck. "Go to sleep."

Ice rimmed the water troughs next morning. "Nip in the air," Speck observed, the words coming out in bursts of frost.

Clint touched his heels to the flanks of his gray, sending the anxious animal up the *calle* that led to the north road out of town to Santa Fe. At Puchiti, they would cut due east. "Yep, but it'll burn off right fast."

Three hours later, three grizzled cowpokes reined up in front of the sheriff's office. Pete climbed down. He growled at his younger brother. "Joe, you pick us up some supplies across the street. Al, you wait here."

Inside, a middle-aged anglo looked up from behind a desk.

Pete grunted. "You the sheriff?"

"Nope. Deputy. Sheriff's over to Atrisco across the river. Expect him back late this afternoon."

Muttering a curse, Pete studied the deputy. "Any strangers come though the last few days?"

The deputy chuckled. "Every day, Mister."

"I'm looking for a family member, a cousin. He's got a thick beard and a scar across his cheek here," he said, drawing his finger from the tip of his ear to the corner of his lips. "Hair don't grow on it, so you can't help seeing it."

Shaking his head, the deputy replied, "I ain't seen no one like that, but check with the sheriff. He makes it a point to look up all strangers just to make sure they ain't going to cause us no problems."

Pete clenched his teeth, suppressing the anger and rage that had been eating at his insides. He nodded. "Smart man."

"Yep. That's why the town has done elected him three times running now."

With a deferential nod, Pete backed away. "Obliged, Deputy. I'll drop by later."

Outside, Pete swung into his saddle as his younger brother rode up, his saddlebags bulging with grub. "Pete! Pete," exclaimed the younger cowpoke. "They was here. Yesterday. The Mexican who runs the general store sold them some grub."

Anger flashed in the larger man's eyes. "He know where they are now?"

"No. He don't know if they rode out or not."

Pete grimaced, anxious to get on their trail, but the smart move was to wait. See what the sheriff had to say.

Chapter Seven

At Puchiti southwest of Santa Fe, Clint and Speck cut east. El Jardin was a few hour's ride across a sprawling valley to the Sangre de Cristos. Clint eyed the magnificent country ahead of him, knowing he was drawing close to the end of his journey. His heart beat faster in anticipation.

They camped that night in the rugged foothills of the Sangre de Cristos. Clint slept little, wondering what would come of his return to the town in which he had grown up.

He rose early next morning and stirred the banked fire, wanting to pull out well before sunrise.

From time to time throughout the day, Speck glanced at his partner, recognizing the worried anticipation in Clint's steely gray eyes. "Nobody ain't going to recognize you, partner. Shoot fire, you changed a heap in the eight years I knowed you. Back then you was just a smooth-faced kid with a likeable face. Now, you're old and wrinkled and uglier than sin," he added with a grin.

Clint lifted a skeptical eyebrow. "Go to hades," he muttered, himself grinning despite the blood pounding in his temples and his heart thudding against his chest.

Soon he would be home. His eyes narrowed, wondering just what might be waiting there for him.

Mid-afternoon, they rode into the small pueblo of El Jardin, nestled in a lush valley on the slopes of the Sangre de Cristos.

The small pueblo had grown some. Clint guessed a couple dozen new buildings, mostly stone, and a few of logs had been constructed on the outskirts of town. For the most part, the village remained the same.

Ten-year-old memories came flooding back. Clint instinctively laid his hand over his beard, then tugged the brim of his John B. Stetson farther down his eyes.

Unlike most of the pueblos through which they had passed, there was no flood of children swarming around them, hawking everything from leather belts to their sisters; no one trying to drag them into their cantinas; and very few citizens walking the cobbled *calles* of the small village.

"Looks half deserted," Speck muttered, his eyes searching the almost empty streets and the dark windows looking down on them like empty eyes of a skull.

The hair on the back of Clint's neck bristled. Looked like the sheriff in Albuquerque had been right. At first glance, the town didn't appear too hospitable. "Maybe it's *siesta*," he replied casually, but his gray eyes continued to scan the town suspiciously, searching for any unusual attention being paid them.

"I don't like it," Speck muttered. "Not one little bit."

"Just take it easy. Let's get a lay of the land."

"Why don't we just ride on out to his place?"

Clint reined up. He drew a deep breath and tried to still the jitters in his belly. "Sam didn't have a place." He nodded to an adobe brick stable and set of corrals on the corner. "Only that livery yonder. See." He nodded to the faded sign on the side of the stable, COOPER'S LIVERY."

"He still own it?"

With a shrug, Clint reined his pony toward the livery. "Might as well find out," he muttered, dragging his tongue over his lips and steeling himself for the meeting with a man he thought dead for the last ten years.

A wizened old Mexican wearing baggy clothes, a battered *sombrero*, and worn *huaraches* hobbled out to greet them. He smiled obsequiously. "*Dé la bienvenida a mi negocio humilde humilde*."

Speck frowned. "What'd he say?"

Clint nodded to the old man. "He's welcoming us to his place of business." He pointed to the sign. "Cooper?"

The Mexican shook his head emphatically and jabbed his finger into his sunken chest. "No. Me Jorge," he replied, pronouncing it 'Hor-hay'. He gestured to the livery. "*Este poseo*. Me."

"This place is his," Clint explained to Speck. He gestured to their ponies. "*¿Cuánto?*"

Nodding sharply, Jorge held up his spread fingers five times. "*Los centavos veinticinco.*"

"Done," Clint said, dismounting. He fished a couple quarters from his pocket and tossed them to the old man. "Grain water, *si?*"

"*Si, si,*" the old Mexican replied, leading the two horses inside.

Clint followed the hobbling old man inside. "You know an Anglo around here by the name of Sam Cooper?"

A look of surprise flickered in the old man's eyes, but then he gave them a patronizing grin and shrugged. "*No hable ingles.*"

Clint laid his hand on the old man's shoulder. "Cooper. Sam Coop-er," he said distinctly.

With a weak smile, the livery owner shrugged once again. "*Yo no sé atal hombre.*"

Speck grunted. "He sure ain't no help."

Clint watched the old man stable the ponies and dispense grain and water to them. "Well, we got to find out if this Sam Cooper is the one I know. He don't own the livery no more." When he mentioned Sam's name again, he noticed the old man's eyes flicked in his direction.

"Maybe the sheriff," Speck suggested.

"It's worth a try." He addressed the old Mexican. "*Señor*, the sheriff?" He pointed to his chest. "Sheriff. Lawman."

The frown on the old man's face faded into understanding. He grinned. "*Si, si. El representante de la ley.*"

He pointed down the street. "*Allí. Abajo allí. Señor* Hitch Faber. There, down there."

The cobbled *calles* were so narrow that two or three times, Clint and Speck were forced to sidle up to one of the stone buildings as a *carreta* rattled past hauling crates of squawking chickens or squealing hogs.

In the next block, they found the sheriff's office. The name, Hitch Faber, was familiar, but Clint couldn't remember if it were from El Jardin or one of the numerous towns through which he had drifted.

Clint approached the sheriff's office warily, hoping no one could see through his beard and the extra twenty pounds manhood had put on him over the last eight years.

Inside, a burly jasper with a heavy plaid shirt drawn tightly over his wide shoulders frowned up at them from behind a desk. A badge was pinned to his vest. In a far corner of the jail, four cowpokes sat around a card table, dealing poker. They looked around as Clint and Speck entered. One looked familiar.

Clint cleared his throat. "Sheriff Faber?"

The hombre at the desk narrowed his eyes. For a moment, he stared up at Clint. A faint frown flickered over his square face, then vanished. He replied, "That's me. What do you want, stranger?"

The sheriff's face brought back no memories.

At that moment, the door to the cellblock opened and a young Mexican *señorita* stepped out. In a hesitating, meek voice she whispered, "The cells, they are clean, *Señor* Sheriff."

"About time. Before you go, don't forget to bring in some wood for the stove. It's going to be a cold night."

She nodded hurriedly and slipped from the office. The sheriff turned back to Clint. "All right, now. Like I asked you, what do you want?"

Remembering the sheriff's warning back in Albuquerque, Clint introduced them and explained. "Just passing through to Denver, Sheriff. Thought we might stop in and pay a short visit to an old friend, Sam Cooper, who lives around here somewhere. Figured you might know where we might find his place."

The door opened, and the young woman scurried in with an arm-load of split kindling. She stacked it by the stove.

Faber's eyes narrowed, ignoring her. His broad jaw grew hard. "Sam Cooper you say?" He studied them a moment, then shook his head. "Nope. I don't know of no Sam Cooper around here." Without turning his head, he spoke over his shoulder. "What about it, boys. Any of you ever heard of a Sam Cooper around hereabouts?"

"Nope. Not me. Never heard of him," was their answer.

"Sorry, gents," the sheriff replied, a faint gleam of amusement in his black eyes. "Reckon someone steered you wrong."

Clint glanced at the jaspers around the poker table. Two of them grinned like possums. The other two stared at the cards in their hands. One of the two, he recognized as a no-account saddle tramp who had frequented the cantina down the street from the livery when Clint was a young man.

He would have laid odds they were lying. "Reckon you're probably right, Sheriff," he said, turning to leave.

Speck started to question the sheriff further, but Clint laid his hand on his partner's arm. "Let's go, Speck. We've taken up enough of the sheriff's time."

"Hold on there, cowboy," Sheriff Faber called out.

Clint looked around, his muscles suddenly tense as cold-rolled steel.

Faber frowned. "You look familiar. Do I know you?"

From the corner of his eyes, Clint saw Speck stiffen. He forced a grin. "Afraid not, Sheriff. We're from over Tucson. Heading up to Denver and thought to stop in for a visit with Sam, but, since he ain't around here, I reckon someone sure steered me wrong." Without giving the sheriff a chance to reply, he touched his fingers to the brim of his Stetson. "Appreciate it anyway, Sheriff."

Chapter Eight

Outside the adobe office, Speck spun on Clint. "They was lying, Clint. I could see it in their eyes."

"Sure they was, but remember what Sheriff Aleman back in Albuquerque told us. I reckon one of the old boys who runs this town is the sheriff. We're not going to find out nothing in there." He looked up and down the narrow *calle*. "Tell you what. Let's find the nearest cantina and then a spot for the night. Maybe if we ask around enough, we can find out what we want. That satisfy you?"

Clatter Dowd watched from the window of the sheriff's office as Speck and Clint ambled down the narrow street and turned into the cantina on the corner. "They went in Pablo's," he said, rolling a cigarette and touching a match to it.

Sheriff Faber grunted. "Reckon they wasn't satisfied with my answer."

John Drucker studied the closed door. "That bearded gent looks familiar, Sheriff. Mighty familiar."

Faber grew thoughtful. "I thought he did, but I can't place him."

Keeping his eyes on the doorway to Pablo's, Clatter spoke over his shoulder. "Want me to find out what they're up to, Hitch?"

Faber opened a desk drawer and pulled out a bottle of tequila. "You and Scruggs mosey on down there. If you got to, explain to them two boys that it would be good for their health if they moved on out to Denver soon as they can. We just about got Cooper where we want him. We don't need nobody butting in. If they don't get the message, then you know what to do."

"What if they find out where the old man's place is?"

"What good's it going to do them? He ain't out there no more."

"Yeah, but they might figure on riding out there anyway."

The sheriff snorted. "Well, you know what road they got to take. Wait for them, but make sure no one finds them."

A crooked grin spread over Dowd's hatchet face. He nodded to George Scruggs who was still seated at the poker table. "Let's go. See if we can encourage them jaspers to look after their health."

Scruggs laughed and shoved back from the table.

"Might as well. Been right boring around here the last few days."

As the door closed behind them, Sheriff Faber glared at the young Mexican girl. "Ain't you finished yet?"

She ducked her head and backed up several steps. "*Si, Señor Sheriff*. I finish." She reached behind her for the door. "I come back in the morning, *si?*"

"Yeah," he growled. "Early."

Clint paused inside the cantina door to accustom his eyes to the darkness.

Flickering candles punched dim holes in the shadows of the saloon, casting eerie shadows on the dingy walls and the canvas ceiling sagging with dirt. A handful of peons in baggy shirts and pants with worn blankets over their shoulders sat around three rough-hewn tables in front of the adobe fireplace in one corner sipping *pulque*.

A middle-aged Mexican thin as a bed slat grinned at them from behind the plank bar. "*Buenos días, Señors.*"

Clint nodded as he bellied up to the wood plank bar. "Howdy."

The proprietor pulled a full bottle of tequila from under the bar. "You want drink, *Señors?*"

Speck glanced around the dimly lit room as Clint nodded and held up two fingers.

"*Si, si,*" exclaimed the obsequious bartender, quickly filling two tumblers to the brim. His black eyes flashed in the candlelight, and his broad grin revealed several gaps in his teeth.

In one quick motion, Clint downed the shot and

dragged the back of his hand across his lips and tossed a gold eagle on the bar. "You speak English?"

The proprietor's eyes grew wide at the gold coin. He reached for it. "*Si*. I speak English good."

Before he could retrieve the coin, Clint grabbed his hand. "I'm looking for Sam Cooper. You know him?"

At that moment, the door opened.

The laughing by the fire ceased.

The bartender glanced over Clint's shoulder, and the grin faded from his face. He shook his head. "*No señor. Yo no hablo ingles.*"

Clint and Speck exchanged sharp glances as Dowd and Scruggs entered the dingy room. The two deputies sidled up to the bar. Clatter jabbed a finger at the bartender. "Give us a drink, Pablo. Stop annoying these cowboys, you hear?" With a leering grin, he added, "They got to be moving on soon as they can."

The bartender's eyes grew wide with fear. "*Si, si,*" he muttered, hurriedly pouring two drinks.

Scruggs turned to Clint and Speck. With a sneering smirk on his pan-shaped face, he said, "You got to watch these greasers. They'll lie when the truth is better, but I'll teach him a lesson."

The bartender ducked his head, but before he did, Clint saw a flash of anger in the smaller man's eyes. "Thanks, friend," Clint said, resisting the urge to slam a fist between the sneering deputy's eyes. He stepped back from the bar. "Appreciate the advice, but it's been my experience that if you give a lesson in meanness to a man or critter, he just might learn that lesson."

Scruggs frowned, failing to comprehend the insult Clint hurled at him.

Two or three peons by the fire snickered.

Clint glanced at Speck. "Reckon it's time we pick up our ponies and ride on out, partner. Make a few miles before the sun sets," he added for the benefit of Scruggs and Dowd. Nodding to the gold eagle on the bar, he grinned at the bartender. "*Gracias, amigo.*"

A look of gratitude filled the old man's eyes. "*Gracias*," he replied. "*Mucho gracias.*"

Moments after Speck and Clint left the cantina, Scruggs and Dowd followed. As soon as the door closed behind them, the young Mexican woman from the jail rushed up to the bartender and whispered in his ear. He nodded, then quickly slipped out the back door and hurried after Clint and Speck.

A voice from the shadows of the livery stopped Clint just as he hitched his foot into the stirrup. "Who's there?" He called out.

The middle-aged bartender emerged from the darkness. "It is I, *Señor*, Pablo. I come to warn you."

Clint lowered his foot and arched an eyebrow. "The bartender?" With a wry grin, he said, "I thought you *no hablo ingles*."

Speck grunted. "Yeah."

With a slight shrug, the thin Mexican replied. "Sometimes, *Señor,* one must forget *ingles*. But, now, I speak the *ingles* good."

"All right, so you speak it good. What do you want with us?"

"If you seek *Señor* Cooper, *Señors*, the sheriff will have you . . ." He searched for the word. "Ah—" He snapped his fingers two or three times in an effort to remember the right word. "Ah, matado, *señor.* Killed."

"What!?" Speck exclaimed.

"You know where Cooper is?" Clint demanded of the Mexican bartender.

Looking into the dark shadows of the livery fearfully, he nodded. "*Si.* The east road to the Pueblo Pecos. Where the road forks beyond the *playa.* That is the way to his *rancho*, but he is not there."

Clint frowned. "Not there? Where is he? How do I find him?"

Pablo smiled slyly. "Do not worry, *Señor.* He will find you, but it is not wise now to take the road to the Pecos. They will wait for you on the road."

"They?"

"The men of the sheriff. Even now, the two in the cantina are watching. They will wait on the road. *Quien sabe*," he added with a shrug. "Perhaps, many, *muchos más.*"

Speck frowned at Clint. "How many jaspers does the sheriff have working for him?"

Pablo held his hands out to his side. "*Mucho.* The sheriff and *el alcalde*, *Señor* Rawlings, they have many *gringo vaqueros.*"

Clint scratched absently at the scar on his cheek. "The

mayor's job too, huh?" He glanced at Speck. "Looks like the sheriff down in Albuquerque knew what he talking about."

"Looks that way," Speck muttered.

Clint pursed his lips. "Is there another road?"

The bartender shrugged. "There are trails in the mountains, but they are known only by the Indians."

"Indians? What tribe?"

"Who can say, *Señor*? Many have been killed. A small band of Piro Pueblos and Tewar Puel Pueblos live to the north. The Zuni and Jemez, they have all fled the *gringo*."

"Now what, Clint?" Speck asked, frustrated.

"Now what?" Clint drew a deep breath. A wry grin curled his lips. He scratched at the heavy beard on his face. "Now, I wouldn't mind laying these old eyes on Ojo Blanco and his boys, but I reckon that's out of the question, so I figure we got to let the sheriff's boys see us head out for Denver. That way, they'll figure there's no sense to watch the road, and then tonight, we can slip back in and take the east road."

With a wry grin, Speck replied. "Sounds good, but where's the east road?"

"*Por favor, señors.* I, Pablo—I show you. Tonight, I wait for you."

Clint studied the thin Mexican staring up at him hopefully. "Why do you help us?"

Pablo glanced fearfully over his shoulder. "The sheriff, he is not *el hombre bueno*. He and those with him, they take from my people. If we speak out against them, it is *malo* for our families. *El Patron, Señor* Cooper, he is good man."

Speck studied the small man. "Reckon we should take a chance on him, Clint?"

Rolling his broad shoulders, Clint arched a quizzical eyebrow. "I reckon. Where do we meet, Pablo?"

Shaking his head, Pablo whispered. "Do not worry. I will be waiting when you come back to El Jardin."

From the dark windows of a small stone building on the outskirts of El Jardin, Scruggs grunted in satisfaction. He turned to Dowd who was hunched over a battered table nursing a mug of tequila. "Well, them two is gone. Headed for Denver. I reckon Hitch oughta be tickled."

Dowd snorted and scooted closer to the fire. "Just hold on to your horses. Let me know when they top out on the pass over the top of old Baldy."

Scruggs nodded.

Thirty minutes later, Clint reined up on the crest of old Baldy, studying the serrated mountain range stretching northward as far as the eye could see. "Mighty fine country," he muttered eyeing the golden patches of aspen dotting the lush meadows backing up to the thick stands of lodgepole and ponderosa pine forests.

"Reckon so," Speck replied. "Except it gets a heap colder here than it does back in Tucson. Give me nice, hot sweating weather any day to freezing snow and rain."

With a teasing grin, Clint replied. "How do you know

Miss Amy wouldn't like this cold weather? Why, she'd need someone to keep her warm at night."

Speck blushed. "Them Arizona nights get cold enough, partner."

Glancing over his shoulder, Clint studied the small village down in the valley behind them. "Reckon we still got eyes on us, so let's us ride on down the slope apiece and then find a snug hole to curl up in until dark."

"That's it," Scruggs announced as the two figures disappeared over the pass. "Them two is gone."

Dowd turned up his mug and drained the tequila. "Let's tell Hitch."

Chapter Nine

The sun rapidly dropped behind the tall peaks, casting cold shadows over the rugged mountains slopes. Night came early in the high country and with it, a piercing chill that cut through the thin air.

Snug beneath an outcropping of granite and shale with a small fire warming them, Clint and Speck watched as the shadows deepened in the valley below. They filled their bellies with hot coffee and fried bacon with Johnnycakes sopped in leftover grease.

"We'll give them until midnight before we ride out. Those jaspers ought to be drunk or sound asleep by then," Clint announced.

A crescent moon rose over the eastern peaks just before midnight, lighting the narrow road with a ghostly pale light. The mountain air had a chilling edge, with a hint of ice come morning.

Bundled in his Mackinaw, Speck noted the frosty breath emerging from the nostrils of their ponies. He growled, "Blazes, Clint, it's cold, too cold."

Clint grinned woodenly at Speck, realizing that within hours, he could be facing Cooper. But was it his Cooper? The knot in his stomach grew tighter. "And bound to get colder," he replied.

As they approached the small village, a slight figure in white stepped from the shadows of an adobe and motioned to them.

"Pablo," Speck muttered as the figure turned and at a trot, led them in a winding route through the small town. The only sounds in the night were the slapping the Pablo's *hauraches* and the click of the horses' hooves on the cobbled streets.

Ten minutes later, Pablo moved to the side of the road and motioned them to continue. "*Vaya con Dios*," he whispered, holding up a hand.

The winding road led down the rugged slope and onto a huge basin cut by glaciers millenniums past. Beyond, the jagged silhouette of another range of mountains rose into the starry night.

For an hour they rode through lush meadows dotted with stands of aspen until they reached the rocky *playa*.

Speck whistled softly when he eyed the dried-up lake bed, which he guessed was at least two miles in diameter. "I thought we had some big ones back home."

As they rode out of the *playa*, the first traces of false

dawn sent exploring fingers above the serrated ridges of the eastern foothills of Sangre de Cristos.

"That must be the fork Pablo told us about," Clint observed, nodding to a Y in the road ahead.

"How much farther, I wonder," Speck muttered. "My toes are like chunks of ice. I can sure use a cup of hot coffee."

Clint agreed. "Come first light, we'll put together a small fire."

By the time the road began to ascend into the rugged foothills covered with thick stands of lodgepole pine and Englemann spruce, the gray of false dawn had followed the night back to the west.

The road topped a ridge, then dropped down to a shallow water crossing through a narrow stream. The clear water ran cold and swift, bubbling and swirling about the rocks and boulders in the bed.

"I'd say we pull up here and boil us some coffee," Clint said, nodding to a small clearing beside the road. "Give our ponies a rest and us a chance to stretch our legs."

Speck grinned, the freckles on his face clustering up in patches. "You ain't getting no argument from me. Why—" A sudden beating of wings interrupted him. He jerked around as a tiny Saw-whet owl darted from the limb of a nearby pine and disappeared into forest. Moments later, its raspy call, like a saw being sharpened, echoed through the trees.

Speck looked back around, his face serious. "We best find us another spot, Clint."

Clint paused, still standing in one stirrup and his free leg dangling. "What are you talking about?"

Speck nodded in the direction the owl disappeared. "That owl. You saw him. This ain't a good spot."

With a groan, Clint dropped to the ground. "You're driving me crazy with that superstition nonsense, do you know it?"

"It ain't nonsense," Speck insisted. "You spot an owl in daylight, it's bad luck."

Before Clint could reply, a soft voice from behind said, "*Por favor*, *Señors*. Do not move, or we will be forced to shoot you."

Clint reacted instantaneously. Even before the last word had fallen off the speaker's lips, Clint had dropped to one knee and had both .36s extended and cocked.

The swiftness of his move stunned the four *vaqueros* facing him, momentarily flustering them.

In that split instant before his fingers squeezed the triggers, a gravelly voice broke the brittle tension. "Hold up, *muchachos*. These are not those we seek."

Four Mexican *vaqueros* with Henry rifles faced Clint, their black eyes narrowed with hate and blazing with anger. Speck, at Clint's side, stood motionless, wide-eyed, his gunhand empty.

Before Clint could say a word, the voice spoke again, this time with a touch of curiosity. "Take it easy, Mister. You ain't the one of them we be looking for. *Muchachos*, *baje sus fusiles*."

For a moment, the *vaqueros* hesitated, then reluctantly lowered the muzzles of their Henrys. From the shadows of the fir and spruces behind them, a weather-beaten cowboy in his mid-fifties rode out forking a Spanish mustang. A faint grin played over his thin lips and he moved a wad of tobacco from one cheek to the other.

Clint glanced up at the rider whose hat was pulled low over his eyes, then shifted his gaze back to the *vaqueros*. He remained vigilant as they lowered the muzzles of their rifles.

The old man spoke, his voice a familiar cackle. "You be right fast with them hoglegs, friend. I only seen one man in my life that fast. Years back." He stared down at Clint with cool blue eyes, trying to read behind a ten-year-old mask. "But, I heard he was dead. Turned gunfighter, then got hisself burned up down in Valverde." He pursed his lips and loosed an arc of tobacco onto the ground.

The words hit Clint between the eyes like a singletree. His gaze dropped to the gnarled hand resting on the saddle horn of the gaudy Spanish saddle. The last two fingers were missing. He peered closer into the old man's face. The words stuck in his throat, but finally he managed to force them out. "Sam? Sam Cooper?"

At that moment, a shrill, thin whistle followed by the urgent notes of a thrush cut through the bubbling of the small stream.

The old man jerked around, peering over his shoulder at the granite slabs thrusting high into the sky above. The call came a second time. He spat out his tobacco, wheeled his mustang about and shouted at Clint. "You want to finish this conversation, you best hit that saddle and stay with us. There's going to be trouble around here faster'n you can blink. He dug the large rowels of his Spanish spurs into his pony's flanks. "*Vayamos, muchachos.*"

Sliding his .36s back into their holsters, Clint swung into the saddle and sent his gray up the narrow trail after Speck who was right behind the old man. Behind him came the four *vaqueros*, driving their ponies hard with whips and spurs. The narrow trail was an ascending series of switchbacks twisting through giant pine and fir stretching over a hundred feet into the alpine air, each switchback taking them higher and higher into the Sangre de Cristos.

Several times, they took a side trail until finally they topped out on a broad granite table in front of a large cave with a rock fence three or four feet high blocking the mouth except for three slender poles that were quickly removed to permit their entrance.

Inside, several Mexican *vaqueros* rushed up to the old man. He barked orders. To one tall *vaquero*, he exclaimed, "*Comprende*, Luiz?"

"*Si, el Patron.*" The *vaquero* nodded and departed.

The old man glanced around at Clint and Speck. In a tone that clearly indicated he expected his orders to be followed, he said, "Wait yonder by the fire. I got some work to do." He turned to one of the young *vaqueros* standing beside his mustang and gestured to Clint and Speck. The young Mexican cowpoke nodded emphatically, then hurried in their direction.

"*Por favor, Señors.* I take *los caballos.* There is food and drink at the fire."

Clint dismounted and handed the young man the reins. He nodded to the old man. "Sam Cooper?"

"*Si*, Senor. *El patron.* He is *mucho hombre. Hombre del campo.*"

Wooden benches were dragged up to a heavy table beside the fire, and mugs of hot coffee and platters of steaming hot tortillas and slices of broiled *cabra* magically appeared along with a large wooden bowl of red pepper sauce so hot that not even a mountain stream could quench the heat.

"Is that Cooper?" Speck asked between bites of goat.

Clint grimaced and shook his head. "Looks that way. If he ain't, he's old Sam's twin right down to the missing fingers."

"How long's it been since you seen him?"

"Ten years." He paused. Memories came flooding back.

Speck took a bite of tortilla. "I thought you said he was dead."

Clint paused, then glanced at his partner. "Reckon I did." He hesitated as a thought hit him. "You know, you never asked any questions about that, did you?"

Speck shrugged. "Wasn't none of my business."

A crooked grin played over Clint's bearded face. "That's one of your personal drawbacks, Speck. You're so blasted nosy."

Speck chuckled. "You know where you can go."

Chapter Ten

As the sun slipped behind the lofty peaks of the Sangre de Cristos and shadows spread the chill of the coming night across the slopes, distant gunshots echoed
down the valley. Savoring the warmth of the blazing
fire and the satisfaction of a full belly, Clint and Speck
exchanged puzzled glances.

None of the contingent of Mexicans seemed unduly
perturbed over the gunfire.

A crooked grin played over Speck's face. "They don't
look none too worried, so I don't reckon we should be
either, huh?"

Clint chuckled. "Suppose not."

"How did you come to get hooked up with Cooper
anyway?"

"Sam raised me from the time I was just a younker,"
Clint explained. "Never knew my folks, and he took me

in. He owned that livery back in El Jardin." He shook his head slowly. "I reckon he had his hands full with me from the beginning. That's how he lost those two fingers. The Comanche who had me didn't want to give me up. Even though that Injun chopped off Sam's two fingers with his tomahawk, old Sam and his .36 Navy Colt convinced that Comanche to turn me over to him. Then he taught me to handle a sixgun. I took to it like a weasel to a henhouse. I practiced all the time. He saw what was coming and tried to stop me. Naturally, being young, I knew all there was to know. He was nothing but an ignorant old man who would never do nothing better than run a livery stable."

He paused, staring thoughtfully at the cup of steaming coffee in his gnarled hands. A frown cut wrinkles into his forehead. "We argued all the time. One day, it was the middle of the winter, snow all over the ground, freezing cold when I braced a yahoo in the saloon. He was faster than me. I knew it, but I was too hard-headed. That's when Sam came in." Clint hesitated, feeling the lump in his throat. "He forced the gunnie to go for his gun. He caught two slugs in the chest. Before the gunslinger could turn back to me, I killed him." He shook his head and groaned. "That started my reputation. Some start. Catch a jasper when he wasn't looking. Anyway, they laid Sam out in a coffin. I left that night. I couldn't stand to see them bury him the next morning."

Speck nodded thoughtfully. "And so for the next couple years, you just drifted, huh?"

A wry grin curled Clint's lips. "Reckon so."

"You built some kind of reputation."

Clint rolled his eyes. "They come looking for me. Seems that yahoo I downed had twenty notches on his sixgun. I was too dumb to realize what kind of hole I'd dug for myself."

A clatter of hoofs on granite interrupted them. Clint looked around to see the old man riding up followed by a dozen *vaqueros*.

Cooper swung down from his mustang and despite a pronounced limp on his left leg, hobbled over to Clint. When Clint rose, Cooper grabbed him by the shoulders and seized him in a bear hug. "Blast it, boy, beard and all. I can't believe it. You're a sight for sore eyes. Why, I thought you was dead."

Clint stammered for words. "Me? I thought you was dead. I saw you in your coffin the night before they buried you. After getting you killed, I couldn't stay and watch them throw dirt on you, so I left town."

A lithesome young *señorita* approached Sam with a cup of steaming coffee in her hands. With a rollicking laugh, he took it. "*Gracias, Maria.*" He paused, then grinned wickedly at Clint. "This here is my daughter, Louisa Maria Consuela Cooper."

Clint stared at him in confusion, and Cooper laughed. "I married her ma when the girl was thirteen. Her pa was a chief among the Owinos, an offshoot of the Santa Clara tribe. That was nine years back, but she's as much my own daughter as if she'd been born to me. Maria, this here is Cleve. I told you about him."

Her eyes grew wide with unasked questions.

Cooper chuckled at her surprise. "Yep. I thought he was dead, but he ain't. This here's your brother, Maria. Come back from the dead." He fished in his pocket for a twist of tobacco and tore off a chunk.

For a moment, the svelte young *señorita* glared resentfully at Clint, then quickly dropped her eyes. Cooper waved to a small anteroom off the side of the cave. "Tequila, Maria. *Por favor.*" With a short nod, she vanished into the shadows. He sipped the coffee and gestured to the wooden benches. "Sit, boys. Who's your friend here, Cleve?"

Clint grinned sheepishly. "I go by Clint now. Clint Bowles. Cleve Bollinger is dead." He paused, then continued. "This here ugly galoot is Speck Adams. We been together eight years or so."

Cooper nodded. "Howdy, Speck." He turned his piercing eyes on Clint. "Now, tell me what you been up to."

Clint grinned at Speck, then turned back to the old man. "First, you tell me how you wasn't killed back then. I saw you in the coffin."

The old man removed his battered hat and laid his gnarled hand on Clint's arm. "I just can't believe you're here, boy. It's a miracle. Praise the Lord, it's a miracle."

Clint glanced sheepishly at Speck. "I don't know about miracles, but I'm here. Now, how about you? What happened back there?"

"Well, son, you missed out on all the excitement. If you remember, the weather was colder than a mother-in-law's kiss. So cold that I didn't bleed out like they thought. They built a fire that night to warm theyselves, but it warmed me and I started bleeding. When some-one spotted the blood dripping on the floor, they come to see what was going on, and there I was, breathing just like I was full alive. That's all nobody could ever figure."

At that moment, Louisa Maria returned with a bottle of tequila, the contents of which she generously splashed into their coffee. Sam winked at her. "*Gracias, mi hija pequeña.*"

Clint recognized the endearment. *Mi hija pequeña,* my little daughter.

The young woman ignored Clint and Speck.

Cooper sipped his coffee and sighed contentedly. "Good, mighty good." He closed his eyes for a mo-ment and a dreamy smile played over his lips. Abruptly, his eyes popped open, and he continued. "I was laid up for a long spell. Come spring, I was getting around some." He paused to lift an eyebrow and give Clint a hard look. "From time to time, I heard about you." He shook his head; his face grew grim. "Didn't like what I heard. You built yourself quite a reputation, boy."

Uncomfortable by the old man's gentle rebuke, Clint shot Speck an embarrassed glance. "Well, I wasn't none too proud of it either. You warned me, but I was too hard-headed to listen. I couldn't stop. They wouldn't let me."

Cooper shifted the tobacco to his other cheek. "That's the way it is. Always someone wanting to prove he's better. Well, what happened down in Valverde? You was supposed to have been burnt up to nothing."

Speck and Clint grinned at each other. Cooper frowned. "What the Sam Hill you two grinning at each other over?"

"That's where Speck and me met up," Clint explained. "I was washing the trail dust off me in a hot bath at the local tonsorial parlor where some jasper stole my hog-leg. On the way back to my room to pick up my spare, I got jumped and carved up pretty good. Speck stumbled across me and helped me over to his *jacale.*" He paused and nodded to Speck.

Clearing his throat, the freckle-faced cowpoke explained. "Next morning, word spread around town about a fire. Seems like the gunfighter, Cleve Bollinger, was burned up. The only way they could identify him was by the fancy ivory grips on his Navy Colt in the burned holster on his hip." He sipped his coffee and nodded to Clint. "I didn't know this ugly galoot from Adam. But while he was feverish and out of his head, he said enough that I figured out who he was. A few days later when he got his sense back, I told him about the fire and about everyone figured he was dead."

"So," Clint added. "That's when I decided Bollinger would stay dead." He paused and looked deep into Cooper's icy blue eyes. "I never killed another jasper in a gunfight. Oh, Speck and me was in the war, and I reckon we might have shot up some Yankee bluecoats, but the old days I left behind."

Cooper nodded slowly. "Well, boy, I'm glad to hear

that. Naturally, Yankee bluecoats don't count none, but the rest sure do."

Clint saw the old man's eyes flick to the hoglegs on his hips. "Navy thirty-sixes," he said. "Nothing fancy."

With a relieved grin, Cooper nodded. "So now that brings us up to now. What are you boys doing here?"

"Down in Tucson, we heard that you was having trouble up here. We come to help," Clint announced matter-of-factly.

"Yes, sir," Speck drawled. "And from what little we've seen and heard, you got yourself a strong dose of trouble. Of course, we got no idea just what it is, but I reckon trouble of one sort is as bad as trouble of another."

Sam studied them a moment, shifting the tobacco back and forth in his cheeks. "Well, Cleve—I mean, Clint. I feel like a new man knowing you didn't burn up down in Valverde, and I'm much obliged for the offer, but I can handle the trouble here."

Clint pushed his wide brimmed hat to the back of his head, puzzled at the old man's gentle, but firm refusal of their help. The pieces of the puzzle just didn't fit. Leaning forward, Clint asked. "What's going on, Sam? What kind of problems you got up here? We heard you had a big spread, so what did you run into that made you end up living in a cave like an Injun?"

A frown swept over the old man's face momentarily and then a gust of cold air whipped the flames of the blazing fire in every direction, sending sparks swirling like the vortex of a tornado. Cooper shivered. "Got some weather coming. Let's get deeper inside, boys," he said, rising gingerly to his feet and leading the way to one of the several anterooms off the main cave.

He pushed through a thick bear hide covering an opening. "We got us a regular little *pueblo* of our own back here," he growled, using the toe of his boot to stir up a banked fire in the middle of the small room.

Clint noticed the frown on the old man's face but dismissed it as he entered the room. He looked around. The room was some larger than the adobe he and Speck occupied back in Tucson.

Blankets and hides were spread on the floor against two walls, and as the smoke from the small fire filtered through the tiny crevices in the ceiling, the heat radiated off the rock walls, making a snug and cozy dwelling.

Cooper nodded to the hides. "Sit. And I'll tell you what you asked." He paused, working the tobacco and then loosing a stream into the fire.

Thirty minutes later, Cooper splashed a healthy slug of whiskey into his coffee. "So that's the story. My wife is shot down and eight years of back-breaking work is gone, taken over by two no-good carpetbaggers and a passel of hired killers."

"What do you mean, taken over?"

The old man snorted. "What do you think I mean? They come in with an army of killers and took over my ranch, all twenty-five thousand acres of it. We had to run to keep from getting killed. My wife was dead, and I had my daughter to think about. So we disappeared into the hills, waiting for the right time to go back." He paused and fixed them with a hard look. "And I'll know when that time is right. Now ain't it."

Clint clenched his teeth. "And there was nothing the law could do about it?"

With a wry grin, Cooper grunted. "Rawlings owns the sheriff and the judge. Them two is the law here, and Rawlings got hisself elected *alcalde,* a job that used to mine," he added with a hint of wry humor. "The few federal marshals we've sent for never got here, so we took to the hills, hoping on some kind of miracle." Pausing, he nodded. "They got theyselves a sweet deal. With the law on their side, they run us out. We ain't got the manpower to whip them in a fight. They know that, and they figure that if they just keep possession, sooner or later, we'll pack up and start over somewhere else." He expelled another stream of tobacco and his eyes blazed. "But there, them jaspers is mistaken. I ain't going nowhere."

Dark clouds rolled in from the north, accompanied by a chilling wind as the three Bodine brothers reined up on the crest of the slope overlooking El Jardin. The youngest brother, Joe, shook his head. "Blast it, Pete. There ain't no sense is us going so far out of the way just so you can get back at some cowpoke that you ain't probably never going to see again. It's crazy!" As soon as the word burst from his lips, he grimaced.

Pete jerked around and glared at his brother. His black eyes glittered insanely. "You calling me crazy?"

Al spoke hastily, "No, he ain't, Pete. All Joe means

is that with all the bad weather coming up, we need to find someplace out of it."

For several moments, Pete stared at his brothers, his broad nostrils flaring. Slowly, then anger seemed to flow out of his massive frame. He rose in his stirrups and glared down at the sleepy pueblo. "The sheriff down in Albuquerque said a jasper who called hisself Bowles and that freckled-face sidekick of his asked about this place. They was looking for some hombre. That's good enough for me." He dropped back in the saddle and touched his spurs to his pony. "Let's ride on down there and see what we can find out."

Al and Joe shook their heads at each other. One of these days, Al told himself, those crazy ideas of his brother's was going to get one of them kilt dead.

Chapter Eleven

The north wind howled down the narrow *calles* and screamed around the corners of the stone and adobe brick buildings as Pete and his brothers reined up in front of the sheriff's office. The razor edge of the vicious wind cut clear to the bone.

Their fingers growing numb, the brothers fumbled to tie their ponies to the rail and hurry through the heavy wood slab door into the jail, where a blazing fireplace in the middle of one wall welcomed them with its satisfying warmth.

To one side of the adobe fireplace, four men looked up from their poker game. Sheriff Faber grimaced, and he shouted. "Close the blasted door, cowboys. This ain't no stable."

Joe grinned sheepishly and closed the door behind them. Pete rolled his broad shoulders. Belligerently, he growled, "I'm looking for the sheriff." He saw that four jaspers wore badges.

Faber leaned back in his chair. "I'm the sheriff."

With a curt nod, Pete said, "I'm looking for a jasper who might have come through here. Wears a heavy beard. Name's Bowles. He's riding with a freckle-faced hombre who's skinnier than a mesquite post."

Scruggs and Dowd exchanged a knowing glance, a move not lost on Pete. Faber remained silent, studying the grizzled cowpoke looking down at him. "Why are you looking for him?" He finally asked.

Pete's eyes narrowed. His reasons were his reasons, nobody else's. He stilled the surge of anger rushing through his veins and stroked his beard. "Personal, Sheriff, Personal."

Nodding slowly, Faber replied. "He ain't here. He headed out to Denver."

"Denver, huh?" He studied the square face of Sheriff Faber suspiciously, wondering if he was deliberately lying or if Bowles had indeed ridden on to Denver. "Hard to believe. What . . ."

Dowd jumped to his feet, knocking his chair to the floor and laying his hand on the butt of his sixgun. "You calling the sheriff a liar, Cowboy?"

Bodine's eyes were no more than thin slits as he glared at the lawman confronting him. Blood pounded in his temples. He was ready to explode. His fingers trembled above the butt of his sixgun, but he managed to keep a rein on his temper. Slowly, he shook his head. "Not me, Mister. I was going to say that we'd been told he was come here to this here town looking for some jasper."

Faber pursed his lips. He studied the three hombres bundled in Mackinaws with worn gunbelts strapped around their middles. "Yep, you're right about that. He come through, like I said. But the old boy he was looking for ain't around here. Never has been. So, him and his sidekick rode on to Denver." He glanced at Scruggs and nodded.

Scruggs hooked his thumb at Dowd. "Me and Dowd here watched them two until they disappeared over old Baldy back north on the Santa Fe-Denver road."

Bodine nodded tersely. "Mind if I ask when that was?"

"Last night," Dowd replied, still facing Pete.

Studying the sheriff and his deputies a few seconds longer, Bodine decided they were telling him the truth. "Much obliged, Sheriff. No offense intended." The last remark was a lie. Pete didn't give a hoot one way or another what the sheriff thought, but the last thing he needed now was trouble to delay him.

The wind howled under the door. Pete continued, "Weather's getting a mite touchy, it appears. You got somewhere around here we can bed down for the night?"

"Down the street is a livery. Next door is a cantina. Old Pablo will let you throw your soogans on the floor in front of the fireplace for a few pesos."

After stabling their horses at the livery, the Bodines stomped through the falling snow to Pablo's where they gathered around a table near the fire and enjoyed a glass of tequila while waiting for a heaping platter of tortillas and peppered red *frijoles.*

Three or four other customers sat around the fire, soaking up the heat.

When Pablo slid the order of *frijoles* and tortillas on the table, Pete grunted and slapped several extra pesos down on the table. "Hey, *muchacho.* I'm looking for a cousin of mine. He's got a large beard and a scar on his face like this." He drew the tip of his finger across his right cheek from ear to lip. "We was supposed to meet here in town."

Pablo hesitated, then eyed the money. "Si, *Señor.* He come here."

Pete winked at his brothers. "I ain't seen him in a long time. He in town here?"

Pablo shook his head and pointed east. "He take road to Pueblo Pecos. He go see *Señor* Sam Cooper."

Al muttered excitedly. Pete shot him a warning look, then reaching for a tortilla, casually replied. "This Sam Cooper. I reckon we can find him over at Pueblo Pecos, huh?"

"No, *Señor.* His rancho is south of the pueblo. The road forks just beyond the *playa.* That is the road you take."

"How far is it?"

"A few hours ride, but as I tell your cousin, *Señor, el Patron*, he is not there."

Bodine's brows furrowed in puzzlement. "Where is he?"

The small Mexican shrugged and made a sweeping

gesture to the mountains around them. "He lives out there, *Señor.* He will find you along the road."

Remembering the sheriff's assertion that the jasper Bowles sought had never been in the area, Pete casually asked, "This Cooper hombre. He been around here long?"

The bone-thin Mexican nodded early. "*Si, Señor. Señor* Cooper, he be here longer than I, Pablo, can remember."

Bodine grunted, wondering just why the sheriff had lied to him.

Speck leaned back against the granite wall of the cave and rolled a cigarette, paying little attention as Clint and Sam reminisced over the past.

The small fire warmed the room, a full belly and powerful whiskey settled a great lassitude over the lanky cowboy's muscles. Despite the howling wind outside and the occasional gusts fluttering the edge of the bear hide covering the doorway, he was growing drowsy.

His mind drifted back to Tucson and the blond tresses and bright smile of Amy. Yep, he promised himself, once he got his worthless carcass back to Arizona Territory, he figured on asking her pa for her hand in marriage. They'd settle down in Tucson, and Clint would take the station manger's job in Yuma. The sound of his name cut into his reverie. Speck sat up. "You say something to me?"

Clint glanced over his shoulder. "No. Go back to dreaming about your little filly."

"I heard my name mentioned."

"Yeah. I told Sam here that you and me had wondered about those gunshots we heard this afternoon."

Curious now, Speck leaned forward. "Yeah. What were they? Trouble?"

Old Sam gave him a wry grin. "And then some. They was Faber's boys."

"Faber? The sheriff?"

"One and the same. His boys was trying to run off a Mexican family down on the eastern slope." He chuckled. "We got there before they got the job done. Sent two of them no-account jaspers hopping over the coals of hades." He paused, then added, "Sometimes we get lucky."

Clint studied the old man who raised him, puzzling over the last remark. Maybe the old man was growing old. He had aged more like twenty years than ten, but his blue eyes remained as clear and determined as the first time Clint saw him facing down that Comanche. "How long's all this been going on?"

Sam sipped his coffee. "Three, four years now since Rawlings came to El Jardin. Faber had been around a spell longer, and the two hooked up. Rawlings started buying up land. To everybody's surprise except Rawlings, Faber got hisself appointed sheriff by Judge JB Hyde."

"So the judge is in on it too?"

The old man eyed Clint a moment, then nodded. "Yep. Them three, they's so crooked they could eat nails and spit out corkscrews."

At that moment, Maria Louisa entered the room with another platter of broiled *cabra, frijoles,* tortillas, and blistering hot red peppers. She sat them on a flat boulder that served as a table.

Clint studied her as she glided around the room. A sister! Well, not really, not by blood. But still, it was a strange feeling knowing that somewhere there was someone he could call family besides Sam.

Sam smiled at her. "Much obliged, little girl," he said gently before turning back to Clint. "And then when the government signed the treaty in June that let the Navahos go back to their land up in Arizona and New Mexico Territory, Rawlings and Faber started running out what few little ranchers was left hereabouts."

Clint pulled out a bag of Bull Durham and began rolling a cigarette. "What did the treaty have to do with it?"

The young woman glanced at Clint and muttered words under her breath to her father.

Sam chuckled. "Be patient, Maria. Cleve—I mean, Clint, he ain't familiar with what's going on around here. You remember, he's been gone ten years." He grinned at Clint. "And ten years has changed things a heap around here."

Despite his ears burning at the look she gave him, Clint ignored her. "So, Sam, like I asked. What about the treaty?"

"Since around sixty-one or two, Navahos and Mescalero Apaches has been kept down at Bosque Redondo on the Pecos River. Used to be a trading post."

He paused to take a sip of his whiskey-laced coffee. "Well, the treaty last June did away with the reservation. The Mescaleros had already run off, but them Navahos, even if they is Injun, they's good, law-abiding folks. Anyway, they went home. A heap of them come through here, but as soon as Rawlings and Faber saw all that land open up down there on the Pecos, they grabbed for it."

Clint studied the old man. "I reckon this is good country for ranching, but an hombre can only keep watch over so much. What else are they after?"

Cooper sighed. "Everyone knows of the gold and silver hereabouts. But lately, copper has been showing up, and now, word is that the Atchison, Topeka, and Santa Fe Railroad was going to buy up right-of-ways." He paused, studying the two cowpokes in the flickering light. "I've done a heap of thinking on it. Faber, he's just a dumb sheriff, but Rawlings—well, that gent is a thinker. The judge too. I figure maybe both of those old boy's got some stake in the railroad. I don't know what it is, but with all that land available, Rawlings could be figuring on becoming a mighty powerful man. And I ain't just talking about New Mexico Territory."

Clint studied him a moment. "You can't be serious."

Cooper shrugged. "Why not?"

"You ain't talking about—" The words refused to roll off Clint's lips. "That's crazy."

Old Sam cackled. "Not so crazy."

"Yeah, but—" He hesitated.

"Go ahead, boy. Say it."

Speck frowned at Clint. "Say what? You two ain't making no sense at all. What's this Rawlings jasper got in mind?"

"President," Clint replied.

Speck frowned. "President? Of what?"

Shaking his head, Clint blew slowly through his lips. "President of the United States."

Late that night, Joe lay in his blankets on the cold stone floor in front of the fireplace, staring up at the reddish glow of the flames dancing on the sagging canvas ceiling.

He always dreamed of being on his own, away from his brothers, away from the sudden anger and rage of his older brother. Still, he felt a tinge of guilt at those thoughts for after all, Pete was his brother, and family stuck together. That's what his pa had always preached before he was hung.

Though he tried his best not to think about it, Joe had the deep-seated premonition that one day, Pete would take on someone he couldn't whip, couldn't bully. And from the look in Bowles' eyes back at Cooper Springs, Joe had the feeling he was the one.

Someone was bound to get themselves killed, real soon, and he hoped it wasn't Pete or himself or Al.

Chapter Twelve

Clint couldn't sleep. He lay awake staring at the flickering light playing over the ceiling, worrying over Sam's plight and trying to figure out why the old galoot had refused help.

During the early hours of the morning, he rolled out of his blankets and slipped into his boots, figuring a healthy dose of fresh air might clear his thoughts. He couldn't help grinning when he saw Speck's worn boots sitting neatly together with toes pointing east–his way of warding off any evil that might come during the night.

Shaking his head, Clint eased from the anteroom into the larger cave where the mustangs milled about. Outside, the clouds were breaking, and the storm seemed to be lessening, but the wind still whipped around the mouth of the cave. Clint rolled a Bull Durham, turned his back to the gusting wind and touched a match to it.

Throughout the night, he had considered old Sam's problems, and any way he sliced the pie, the only thing he could find was trouble, big trouble. If Rawlings and his henchman were as deeply entrenched in the territory as Sam claimed, then the repercussions of prying their greedy fingers from their ill-gotten gains would reverberate throughout New Mexico Territory.

So, why didn't Sam want help? He was no match for Faber and Rawlings. By his own admission, he faced an army of gunhands. He knew what the odds were. He wasn't senile so why refuse Clint's offer?

The rawboned cowboy ground the butt of his cigarette under his heel and stepped outside. The cold wind stung his face. Overhead, the thick clouds rolled and tumbled.

He crunched through the snow to a pine on the edge of the granite plateau. Huddling down in his heavy Mackinaw, he leaned against the scaly bark and peered unseeing into the darkness of the valley below, pondering the situation.

Maybe the old man was right when he claimed he didn't need any help, Clint told himself. *Maybe, I just ought to pack up and ride out. Let the dead stay dead.* "Besides," he muttered. "Look at all you could be throwing away if the law finds out that Cleve Bollinger is alive."

Behind him, his gray whinnied. Clint studied the dark mouth of the cave, and for several excruciating minutes, struggled with the overpowering urge to saddle up his gray and head back to Arizona Territory.

He took a deep breath and released it slowly. Shaking his head, he muttered, "That's the smart move, Clint. After all, you've got your own life. You spent the last eight years making it right."

The wind slackened. He peered into the heavens. Through the swaying pine tops, the fresh, glistening faces of the bright stars shone through the breaks in the clouds. The storm was dying out, and the skies were clearing.

Suddenly, the faint sound of feet crunching on snow spun him around. Maria, a heavy bear skin draped over her head and wrapped around her shoulders, stood staring up at him. In the pale starlight, he saw the set to her jaw and the slight frown on her face. "My father is pleased you are here," she whispered without feeling.

Sensing her hostility, Clint nodded slowly. "I would have come sooner, but I thought he was dead."

"He said that many times."

Her reply surprised him. "He spoke of me?"

"Yes. Often with tears in his eyes although he tried to hide them from me."

Clint waited for her to continue. When she didn't, he said, "I'm sorry about your mother. Sam told me she had died."

Maria's voice grew hard. "She was murdered by the sheriff. He would kill my father if he could, but the people of the mountains, they say nothing when the sheriff questions them of my father."

Clint couldn't help noticing the emphasis she placed on the words, my father. His eyes swept the mouth of the cave, "You have lived here since then?"

"No. We have many camps such as this. That is why we have always escaped the sheriff." She paused. "But, one day—" her voice trailed off, and she dropped her gaze to the ground. After a moment, she looked up and jerked the bearskin from her head. She glared at Clint. "I do not know why you come. If not to help my father, then it best you go. He has worries enough." She stared at him another few seconds, then turned to leave.

Her words slapped him in the face. "Hold on there," he growled.

She jerked to a halt, facing away from him, refusing to turn around.

He spoke to her back. "He gave me the idea in there that he didn't want any help."

With a sneer across her lips, she turned to face him. "Are you so foolish you do not know why?" Before Clint could reply, she continued, "You were dead to him once. Now you are alive." She shook her head slowly. "He does not want to see you dead again."

He considered her remark. Such a thought had not occurred to him. In the pale starlight, he saw her eyes narrow. "You don't care much for me, do you?"

A crooked smile replaced the sneer on her lips. "No."

"What did I ever do to you?"

She arched an eyebrow. "It is what you did to him."

Clint frowned, puzzled. "And just what did I do to him?"

"You left him. You never concerned yourself of his welfare."

"But, I thought he was dead."

"You should not have left."

Clint shrugged. "Maybe not, but what was I to do?"

She shrugged. "For two years, he spoke of you and the craziness with the gun, and then he heard you were dead."

Stifling the urge to explain, Clint studied her face half hidden by flickering shadows cast by the swaying treetops. "Did he tell you that? About the craziness?"

The young woman glared at him. "He spoke of just what a fine young man you were despite the craziness in your head with the gun." Before Clint could respond, she continued, "I could see the pain in his eyes when he spoke of you. There is no worse pain than the death of a child," she added softly.

Clint had to admit that often in the past ten years, he had thought of Sam, of returning to the old man's grave, but he always found an excuse. The real reason was he did not want to face the cold realization that Sam was in the grave because of Clint's own recklessness.

He set his jaw. "I am here now."

"For how long? It would be best if you and your friend rode out now. While my father still sleeps. The longer you say, the more he will expect, and when you do leave, the pain will be as the strike of a rattlesnake." She paused. "I think all would be much better if you had never come. You have brought memories that awaken the pain that had once been asleep."

"But he doesn't want my help. He said so himself."

She shook her head slowly. "Are you so blind you cannot see he does not wish you hurt?"

He parted his lips to speak, but no words came.

She studied him silently for several seconds, then turned on her heel and headed back into the cave.

Watching her retreating back, Clint absently retrieved the bag of Bull Durham from his shirt pocket and rolled a cigarette. A flush of anger rushed through his veins. He cut his eyes toward the corral where his pony stood watching. Maybe she was right. Maybe everyone would be better off if he returned to Tucson.

A gust of wind blew across his face. He closed his eyes. No! He had run away once because he couldn't face the pain that resulted from his actions. He paused to touch a match to his cigarette. He drew deeply then blew a stream of smoke into the air. No, this time, he would not run. Regardless the cost.

Back inside, Sam and Speck still slept. Clint fed a few branches to the fire. He slid into his bedroll and lay staring at the shadows dancing across the granite roof over his head.

Unanswered questions tumbled about in his head, at times forcing him to doubt the wisdom of the decision he had made. He reminded himself that once committed, once acted upon, there could be no going back. And no one could predict what lay ahead.

"More bark than bite," Sam commented about the storm next morning around a cozy fire as he sipped coffee and chewed on tortillas and goat.

Speck couldn't help noticing that Clint was staring into the fire, unusually quiet. He nodded and replied to Sam's comment. "Fine with me. I ain't too much for cold weather."

The old man cackled, then grimaced as he used both hands to straighten his left leg. "You one of them Arizony boys through and through, huh?"

Speck sipped his coffee. "Reckon I am, Mister Cooper."

"Call me Sam. Everybody does."

"All right, Sam. Yep, I'm all Arizona. When cold weather comes, I'm like a bear. I just want to hibernate until it gets hot enough to sweat." He glanced at Clint. "Ain't that right, partner?"

Clint jerked his gaze from the fire. "Huh? What's that? I wasn't paying no attention."

Speck nodded to Sam. "I was telling Sam there that I liked my weather hot enough to melt a tallow candle."

Clint gave a terse shake of his head. "Yeah. Yeah, I suppose so."

Sam shot Speck a puzzled look at the enigmatic response. It was obvious Clint was considering concerns other than the storm.

Before either could say a word, Maria pushed through the bearskin door and set a platter on the rock table. In the middle of the platter was a large bowl of honey. On one side were stacks of fried corn cakes the size of silver dollars and on the other side, pemmican rolled into balls and held together with grease.

Speck grinned and patted his belly. "I reckon you

was reading my thoughts, Miss Maria," he said with a big grin, reaching for a corn cake. "I was getting so hungry, my tapeworm figured I had gone and shot myself." He dabbed a cake in the bowl of honey and then bit off half the cake.

Clint remained silent, watching her every move, but the young woman deliberately kept her eyes averted. "Much obliged," he said.

Her only response was a short nod of her head.

Clint leaned back and sipped his coffee, studying Sam who was putting himself around several honeyed corn cakes.

He glanced at Speck who was eyeing him warily, expectantly. A crooked grin curled his lips, and he winked at Speck.

The lanky cowpoke rolled his eyes and groaned.

Sam frowned. "Something wrong, Speck?"

Before Speck could reply, Clint spoke up. "Sam, you best eat up. I'd like to take a look at that ranch of yours and try to figure how just how we're going to get it back.

Chapter Thirteen

The early morning sun bathed the snow-covered pueblo of El Jardin with bright sunlight as the Bodines stomped from the cantina and into the livery to saddle their ponies. "Move it," Pete growled at his brothers. "We got a hard ride ahead of us."

At that moment, Sheriff Faber and Deputy George Scruggs paused outside the corral. Bundled in a fur-lined leather coat and his wide-brimmed hat tugged low on his head, Faber called out, "See you boys is getting an early start to Denver."

Pete peered over the saddle as he slid the leather latigo through the cinch ring and tugged it tight. "Reckon you're right about that early start, Sheriff, but not to Denver. We're heading east." He pulled the stirrup off the saddle seat where he had laid it while snugging down the cinch.

Faber stiffened. Puzzled, he glanced at Scruggs before turning back to Bodine. "What's that you say? East?"

Pete swung into the saddle and rode over to the rail. "Yep. After we left you yesterday, we stopped at the cantina there. Little Mexican inside said the ones I'm looking for went east, down south of some place called Pueblo Pecos."

The sheriff's eyes blazed. He stared up at Pete, seeing the smug grin on the bearded hardcase's face. The gleam of amusement in Bodine's eyes told Faber that the grizzled cowpoke figured the sheriff had lied to him in the office the day before. "Pueblo Pecos, huh?"

Bodine's eyes grew hard. "That's what he said. Seems like that jasper you said ain't never been around here lives over there."

Sheriff Faber stared up at the leering cowboy. Over the last few years, working for Rawlings had tempered Faber's impulsiveness for on more than one occasion observing Rawling, the sheriff had witnessed the benefit of a well thought-out response as opposed to belligerent threats.

"Well, I see you stumbled on to my lie," he drawled, giving Scruggs a murderous glare. "Though I was told them two rode to Denver."

Scruggs groaned, and Pete simply nodded.

Faber continued, unperturbed by the discovery of his duplicity. "You in a big hurry?"

Al and Joe rode up beside their brother. "Not especially," Pete growled.

Faber nodded. "I got the feeling yesterday you ain't

looking for this Bowles jasper just to give him a hug. This hombre you're looking for. Mind telling me why you want him?"

Pete shrugged. "I aim to kill him."

The words did not faze Sheriff Faber. To the Bodines' surprise, Faber grinned and replied, "Maybe you and me ain't so far apart after all. Come on over to my office. I got an idea that we can help each other."

Faber and Scruggs walked down the narrow *calle* ahead of the three brothers. Scruggs whispered. "We don't know them jaspers, Sheriff. How do we know we can trust them?"

Faber snorted. "We don't, and we ain't. Now, you get over to Pablo's and find out how come that jasper and his sidekick didn't ride on out to Denver. And make sure that little greaser learns not to talk to strangers no more, you hear? See if you can handle that better than keeping an eye on strangers."

Sheriff Faber hung his heavy coat on a peg in the wall. He turned back to the Bodines and nodded to the adobe fireplace. "Coffee's hot."

The brothers stood motionless, staring at him.

With a shrug, the sheriff poured himself a cup and plopped down at his desk. "I don't know what this Bowles jasper is to you, and I don't care. I got a proposition that'll protect you from territorial law, put a few dollars in your pockets, and let you do whatever you want to that friend of yours. Interested?"

"What's in it for you?"

"Don't worry. I'll get what I'm after. Well?"

"You're the one doing the talking," Pete growled.

"I ain't explaining nothing to you boys except that I'll make you deputies and pay you five hundred dollars each, half now, the other half when the job's done. Now this Bowles jasper is looking for a rancher name Sam Cooper, so while you're putting Bowles on the stairway to hades, send Cooper along with him for company."

Pete pursed his lips. "Cooper? Why?"

Faber shook his head. "That ain't none of your business."

"Take it, Pete," whispered Al, laying his hand on his brother's arm. "Take us two years to make that much *dinero.*"

Pete shook the arm off. He growled, "What's to keep us from doing it anyway? You?"

The sheriff suppressed the surge of anger at Bodine's arrogance. "Not a thing, but I figure you're smart enough to see the advantage of carrying a badge and pocketing five hundred dollars. When you kill Cooper and this friend of yours, it's the law, not a back-shooting killing. That's what's to keep you from doing it anyway."

With a grunt that was half-laugh, half-snort, Pete nodded. "Well, I ain't stupid. Swear us in."

After swearing the three Bodines in as deputies, Faber gave them instructions on how to find the Cooper Ranch. "The *hacienda* is on a hill overlooking the Pecos River." He handed Pete a note. "Give this to Zeke Turner. He's the big augur, the ramrod. He's got twenty ranahans, all top hands, not a saddle warmer among them. He'll tell you about Cooper."

Pete glanced at the note and arched an eyebrow.

Faber chuckled. "Read it if you got a mind. I'm just telling Zeke to do what he can to give you old boys a hand."

Scruggs returned as the three rode out, heading east toward Pueblo Pecos. He nodded to the Bodines. Faber grinned slyly. "If we're lucky, those jaspers will take care of Cooper for us. I'm tired of chasing that old man all over these mountains. Maybe those three can find him. If they get theirselves killed off, no one will miss them." He paused. "Now, what about Pablo?"

"You know these Mexicans. That Pablo claims he didn't say nothing. He swore them two just come in and asked him how to get to Pueblo Pecos." He removed his leather gloves that had bloodstains on the knuckles. "But don't worry. He knows better now than to open his mouth to any strangers."

Back in the cave, Sam froze, his mug of coffee halfway to his lips. He stared at Clint. "What was that you said?"

Maria looked at him in surprise, and Speck just rolled his eyes. Clint fixed his eyes on the old man's. "I know you don't want any help, but I said we're going to get that ranch of yours back."

Sam sputtered. "Just how do you figure on doing that? They got twenty gunhands out there holding the place down."

"How many *vaqueros* can you put together?"

Sam snorted. "None of my *vaqueros* is gunhands."

He glanced darkly at the .36 Navy Colts on Clint's hips. "Not what you call gunhands."

Clint sipped his coffee. "I didn't ask about gunhands. What I asked was how many *vaqueros* can you raise?"

Sam sat up straight and looked deep into Clint's gray eyes. "You're serious, ain't you? You figure on trying to fight Rawlings and Faber." He read the answer in the younger man's eyes. "I told you last night, we was waiting for the right time to go back. This ain't it. They got too many gunnies. I'll know when the time is right."

"When will the time be right, Sam? The longer they keep their hands on it, the harder it's going to be to tear them loose."

The old man sneered. "Keep after this, and you're going to get a heap of hombres kilt, and probably you too. You still got the killing lust inside you, don't you, boy?" His words sizzled with rancor.

Clint winced at the cutting words. His ears burned as he glanced briefly at Maria who was staring at him in surprise. "Everyone dies, Sam," he replied flatly, doing his best to hold his temper.

"No. Not for nothing more than a ranch. It ain't worth dying for," Sam snapped, his brows knit and the wrinkles on his forehead furrowed. "The ranch wasn't worth my wife's life."

For a moment, Clint hesitated, hating to paw at a fresh wound, but he knew that if infection wasn't cleaned out of the wound, it would just keep eating away at the healthy flesh. "So what are you going to do? Spend the rest of your life running from one cave to another like a scared rabbit?" Clint's sharp words chided the old man.

Sam grimaced. "They got us out-gunned. They're too strong for us. If we hit them, and they'll bury every last one of us. We've got to wait. Something will turn up. The law will come in sooner or later, and make things right."

A tiny smile curled one side of Clint's lips. "No, it won't, not soon enough. You said it. Rawlings and Faber got this part of the territory under their thumb, and they'll keep it there unless we stop them. They've got the power now. When the law comes in, it'll go straight to those in power. Can't you see that?" He pushed to his feet. "Now, how many *vaqueros* can you raise?"

A flush of excitement colored Maria's cheeks. She looked hopefully to her father. That's when she saw a flicker of indecision in his eyes.

Before she could speak, he shook his head. "I ain't going to give you no help, boy. It ain't time. Like I said, my *vaqueros* ain't no match for Rawling's hired guns. I ain't going to ask them to get theirselves kilt just because you got a wild hair. Best thing you can do is ride on back to Arizony. Like I said before. I can handle the trouble here."

Stunned by the old man's decision, Speck looked up at Clint as his partner's face grew hard in anger. The bearded cowpoke stood motionless, staring down at

Cooper with cold eyes. "When's that time going to get here, Sam?" Anger and frustration honed a sharp edge on his words. "Nothing's changed at all between us."

The old man glared up at Clint. "Don't you worry none, boy. I'll know when."

Clenching his teeth in an effort to control his temper, Clint cut his eyes toward Maria, then at Speck. "I ain't going to get no help out of this contrary old man. I'm riding over to the ranch to take a look. Was I you, Speck, I'd saddle up my dun pony and head back to that purty little thing in Tucson." He paused and looked back at Sam. "Are you going to send someone to show me where your place is, or do I find it myself?"

Sam glared belligerently at Clint, trying to force his own will on the younger man, but Clint's gaze was too intense. Sam's eyes wavered. "You was always mule headed. That's what got me all shot up in the first place. Well, I ain't going to help you get yourself or anyone else kilt. I might not be able to stop you, but I sure ain't going to help. Find the place yourself."

Clint glared at the old man. "You was always stubborn, never listening to no one. But don't worry. I'll find it."

A soft voice broke the silence. "I will show you."

The three men looked around in surprise at Maria who was staring defiantly at her father.

"Maria!" Sam exclaimed. "No. I forbid it."

A gentle smile played over her soft face. "*Mi padre,* I know the fear you have for your son's life. I, too, fear, but I fear more for you. There is no dignity living in the hole of a rabbit while others live in the *hacienda* you and *mi madre* work so long to build. I must show him the *rancho*."

Chapter Fourteen

"You cannot. I forbid it."

She stared up at him. "I must!"

Clint spoke up. "He's right, Maria. It's too dangerous for a woman. Just point me in the right direction or
send one of your *vaqueros* to show me the way."

Speck unfolded his lanky frame to stand beside Clint.
"Might as well point me in the same direction too, Miss
Maria."

Without taking her eyes off her father, she set her jaw
and replied, "I will show you. I have made up my mind."

Sam's weathered face darkened in anger. A white
rim outlined his tightly compressed lips. He glared at
her, but the young woman, her slight shoulders thrown
back, faced him with steel resolve.

Slowly, the old man's face softened. He touched a
battered finger to her cheek with great tenderness. "*Mi

poco uno. My little one, you have the temper of *su madre.*"

A bright smile blossomed on her face. "*Gracias, mi padre.*"

"Be careful," he whispered. "Do not go beyond *el Pico del Aguila.*" He glared at Clint. His voice snarled with disgust. "From the peak, even he can see the *rancho.*"

With a faint nod, she stepped backward, then quickly left the room. "I will meet you at the corral," she said as she pushed aside the bear skin rug over the door.

Clint turned on his heel and stomped from the room.

Sam spat a stream of tobacco juice into the fire and cursed.

Bundled in heavy furs and mounted on a roan mustang, Maria led the way down the mountain trails and over several ridges before the sun hit the middle of the crisp blue sky.

Clint couldn't help admiring the ease with which she sat her saddle, moving as one with the mustang.

Reining up on the crest of a hogback ridge, she spoke for the first time since the cave that morning. "There, the next ridge is *Pico del Aguila*, Eagle's Peak. From there, you can see the *rancho*. Come."

Eyeing the slope beneath them, Clint said, "We can make it from here."

Maria ignored his words, sending her wiry little mustang down an almost imperceptible trail. Clint looked around at Speck who just shrugged and nodded after her.

Thirty minutes later, they reined up several yards

before the crest of Eagle's Peak. Maria swung down from her pony and ground reined the animal, then clambered on up to the crest. Clint and Speck followed.

Crouching behind a boulder, she nodded to the valley below. "There is our *rancho*, and the *hacienda*." She nodded to a narrow road clinging to the side of the mountain. "That road below leads from the north. Across the valley is the south road to Bosque Redondo and Anton Chico far down the river."

Clint noted that the narrow road twisted and curled along the mountainside, around hogback ridges, through narrow canyons of granite, fording streams, deferring to obstacles thrown up by the forces of nature.

At the bend of the road sat a small log cabin from which a thin column of smoke drifted. Two ponies were standing hipshot in the small corral next to it.

She muttered, "Rawlings has guards on the road. They allow no one in."

"The other road too?" Clint asked.

"*Si.* And there is our *hacienda.*"

Far below on a hill in the bend of the Pecos River sat a two story stone *hacienda* with a parapet roof and its outbuildings in the middle of a sprawling compound surrounded on four sides by a ten-foot high wall of stone.

The countryside around the *hacienda* was covered with a layer of fresh snow, brushed away in places so the great herds of cattle could graze.

Speck whistled softly.

Clint muttered, "Nice. Mighty nice."

Maria shot him a smug, yet pleased smile.

He smiled back. "I don't blame you for wanting this back. It's a mighty fine spread."

"Sure is," Speck remarked, opening his canteen and turning it up.

Clint grew serious. "Best you go on back. This was as far as Sam said you was to come."

Her black eyes flashed. "I do not know what you plan to do, or how you will go about it, but I stay—"

"No, you won't!" Clint interrupted. "You're getting your hide back to the cave. And now!"

She arched an eyebrow. "You do not wish for me to show you the tunnel leading into the storeroom under the *hacienda*?" She asked innocently.

Speck choked on his water. "A—a tunnel?" He looked at Clint in disbelief.

Maria remained silent, smiling smugly at them.

"What kind of tunnel?" Clint asked suspiciously.

"To escape the attack of the Mescaleros if they overran the *hacienda*. That was before they went to the reservation at Bosque Redondo." She pointed to the *hacienda*. "The tunnel runs from a wall panel in the basement storeroom below *la cocina,* what you anglos call the kitchen, to an arroyo that opens onto the river where the entrance is covered with undergrowth."

Glancing down at the *hacienda*, Clint asked, "How do you know they haven't found it?"

A tiny smile ticked up her lips. "The gringos might have run us from our home, but we still watch. The tunnel has not been discovered."

Clint studied her a few moments. "All right. Tell us

how to find it, and then you have to leave so you can get back before dark."

She shook her head. "I cannot tell you. There are several arroyos in the forest there. I must show you. And then I will leave," she replied, smug in the knowledge that the two anglos had no choice.

"How do I know you will leave?" Clint demanded.

With a feigned pout on her face, Maria replied, "As a good Catholic, I cannot lie. Once I show you the proper arroyo, I will leave."

He studied her a moment, perceiving a flickering hint of slyness in her eyes. "And return to your father," Clint reminded her.

Her eyes flashed. A faint smile curled her lips when she realized he had caught her duplicity. She nodded. "*Si. Si.* To my father."

Speck chuckled. "Well, partner," he drawled. "It looks like the little lady's holding all the cards."

Clint studied her several moments, irritated with her stubbornness, yet admiring her determination. "I reckon you're right."

A shale outcropping extended several feet out from the rocky slope, offering a canopy they could remain under until dark. Just before the sun dropped behind the peaks to the west, a whistle from down below cut through the still mountain air.

Clint grabbed his six–gun, but Maria stilled him. "Do no worry. It is Luiz. He is my father's *cargador*, what you call ramrod. He comes to escort me back to the cave."

Speck frowned.

She laughed. "My father sent him. It is his way." She fixed her eyes on Clint's. "He is very jealous of his children's welfare." Her eyes held the rawboned cowboy's for several seconds, then shifted to the approaching rider and added, "Some might think too jealous."

Her words were not lost on Clint.

To Clint's surprise, Maria did as she promised. After guiding them along the tree-lined riverbank and showing them the arroyo that led to the escape tunnel, she and Luiz headed back to the cave, leaving Clint and Speck in the foothills just beyond the snow-covered pastures of the *hacienda*.

As the couple disappeared into the thick stands of lodgepole pine on the foothill slopes, Speck muttered. "You think she's really going back?"

Clint chuckled. "She said she would."

With a wry cackle, Speck said, "You believe her?"

He studied the forest she and Luiz had disappeared into. "You know, I think I do."

Speck sighed. "So now what?"

"Now, we find us a spot where we can keep a watch on this place for a few days. Let's find out exactly what we're facing."

Other than a few brief snow flurries, the next couple days passed uneventfully. From a snug camp on the southern slope of the mountain, they had a panoramic view of the entire valley, watching several riders come and go from the *hacienda*. Few of the cowpokes gave the appearance of wranglers but instead, as Sam had claimed, of gunfighters.

Lying on their bellies on the outcropping and surveying the *rancho* the second afternoon, Speck studied the two hardcases on the road below riding out to relieve the two night guards at the south road cabin. "They seem mighty intent on guarding them roads," Speck muttered.

Clint chuckled. "That's good news for us, bad news for them."

"How many gunhands you figure are down there, Clint?"

"Twelve, fifteen. Maybe as many as twenty." He paused and a cruel grin played over his bearded face. "It's about time we find out just how many and how stubborn they are about staying around."

Speck hoisted himself to his elbows. "Well, from the looks of it down there, the river's about a quarter mile from the *hacienda*, which means we're going to have us a long walk through that tunnel."

A wry grin twisted Clint's lips. He rubbed the scar on his cheek. "That's exactly what I was thinking." He pushed to his feet. "You keep an eye on things here. I'll be back."

Speck frowned. "Where you going?" he asked suspiciously.

Clint nodded to the two hardcases disappearing up the south road. "I think I'll see just how determined those old boys are to hang around."

Tagging well behind the two riders, Clint pulled into

a thicket of buckbush when they reined up at the log cabin beside the road. Moments later, two other cowboys emerged, saddled their ponies in the small corral adjoining the cabin, and headed back to the *hacienda.*

Clint studied the cabin for fifteen minutes, then rode up to the log structure, halting in front beside the two saddled ponies and calling out, "Hello."

The door opened and two rawhide-tough hardcases wearing low-hanging six–guns ambled out, looking at Clint with a sneer on their lips. "You must have lost your way, Cowboy. You don't belong around here."

The second jasper chuckled.

Clint grinned, but his words were colder than a Wyoming well digger. "Funny. That's exactly what I was going to tell you old boys. In fact, I can promise you that if you want to see the sun go down tonight, you best fork those ponies and head out for Bosque Redondo–and don't look back."

The sneer faded from their lips. The first one muttered, "Sounds like a threat to me, Cowboy."

"Not a threat, partner. A promise." His eyes narrowed. "Now ride out or make your play."

In the blink of an eye, the first hired gun grabbed for his sidearm but before he cleared leather, Clint's .36 spit out yellow fire, slamming an eighty grain slug into the stunned owlhoot's shoulder, smashing it and sending him spinning to the ground.

The second hired gun threw up his arms. "Not me, mister. I ain't drawing against you. Not me."

Clint peered at him through the pall of gunpowder

smoke. "Throw your partner on his pony and ride out. Don't come back."

"Don't worry. I ain't." He started for the cabin.

"Hold it," Clint barked.

"But, I got some gear—"

Clint cocked the .36. "You got a choice to ride out now or not at all."

The cowboy gulped, slid his arm around his groaning partner's chest and helped him into the saddle. "I'll be watching this road," Clint said. "Don't come back."

After the two disappeared around a bend in the road, Clint headed back to their temporary camp, detouring for a few minutes to find a more permanent hidey-hole. He rode up to Speck as the sun was beginning to drop. "Grab your gear. Let's ride. We got a busy night ahead of us."

Speck nodded to the road. "I heard a shot."

A crooked grin played over Clint's lips. "One of them needed a little prodding. That's all. Now, let's ride. I found us a snug spot to hole up in. Then we'll take care of our friends down at the *hacienda*."

"What you got in mind?"

The rawboned cowboy shrugged his broad shoulders. "Who knows? Play it by ear. At least, we'll get us a better idea of what we're up against."

Thirty minutes later, after pushing through a new growth of white fir into a narrow arroyo ascending the slope, they dismounted in a cave a mile south of the *hacienda*. They stabled their ponies around the first bend in the cave, built a fire, and roasted two rabbits Speck snared down by the small stream at the base of the slope.

While Speck tended their supper, Clint roamed the forest around the cave, searching for dead pine—filled with pitch it made an excellent torch.

Before sundown, the clouds blew away, promising a clear night. At midnight, Clint and Speck slipped out of the cave. The starlight reflected off the snow, making the ride easy. They made their way around the edge of the forest to the river and followed the shore upstream to the mouth of the arroyo which was covered by a thicket of dried bunchberry vines with layers of carpetweeds heavy with white blooms.

After easing through the carpetweeds, Clint led the way up the winding arroyo to the entrance to the tunnel.

The mouth was covered with spider webs layered with snow. Clint held out the torch. "Ready?"

Speck cleared his throat. "I suppose."

"You run across any good luck signs today," Clint asked, still staring at the spider webs and the dark hole behind them.

"Saw a tree swallow on a limb," Speck croaked.

Clint frowned. He glanced over his shoulder. "I didn't know that was good luck."

"It ain't, but it ain't bad luck either."

With a groan, Clint knocked the webs aside and plunged into the tunnel. Once inside, he struck a match to the foot-long shard of lighter pine.

Chapter Fifteen

By the pale light flickering on the rocky sides of the cave, Clint saw the tunnel was man-made, laboriously cut out of stone and shored by heavy timbers

Within ten minutes, the dim torchlight flickered on the end of the tunnel and a flight of rough hewn steps led upward.

Without a word, they gingerly climbed the steps. "Here's the panel," Clint whispered, handing Speck his torch and gingerly easing the slab of rough wood open a crack. No light shone through, so he pushed it open and stepped inside.

The storeroom was blacker than a blacksmith's apron. The small torches punched tiny holes in the darkness, allowing the two cowpokes to pick their way between rows of shelves laden with earthen jars, various food-stuffs, and miscellaneous supplies. In addition to the shelf goods, they found slabs of salted pork and wooden barrels filled with congealed hog grease containing cured hams.

Clint jerked to a halt and held the torch closer to a shelf on which sat three wooden crates, each with three black Xs stamped on them. Peering inside, Clint grinned, and quickly slid a box from the shelf and opened it.

"What is it?" Speck asked.

Gently, Clint picked up foot-long cylinder wrapped in oilpaper. "Dynamite," he muttered, studying the stick. "I heard some talk about it in Tucson. Use it now instead of black powder for blasting. Some foreign jasper come up with it last year, so I hear." Then he had idea. He slipped the stick into the pocket of his Mackinaw. "Take this case over to the tunnel while I find some fuses."

"Fuses?" Speck frowned.

Clint explained. "From what I heard, fire sets the dynamite off. Stick a fuse in it and light it. That's all there is to it."

By the time Speck carried the dynamite to the tunnel and returned, Clint had jammed a large coil of fuse into his pocket. He motioned Speck to follow as he led the way along the row of shelves to a solidly constructed flight of stairs leading up to the kitchen. Silently, he opened the door to the kitchen.

Flickering oil lamps from the adjoining salon cast dancing shadows into the kitchen, or *cocina* as the locals called it. The *cocina* was typical of many finer *haciendas* with two large fireplaces against one wall. A small fire flickered in one. In the other fresh kindling was stacked for the morning fire. In the middle of the room sat a ponderous table around which half-a-dozen *cocineros* could prepare meals. The room was deserted, so Clint slipped in with Speck on his heels.

Peering around the door-jamb to the adjoining room, Clint noted that a cold fireplace anchored one corner of the salon, a large room where the family entertained. In front of the fireplace were several sturdy chairs behind which a heavy table sat on the flagstone-tiled floor, surrounded by a dozen equally heavy chairs. Around two walls ran heavy wooden benches under which were several leather chests and earthen jars. On one of the two walls was mounted a dark mantel that held a Regulator clock, several handguns, boxes of cartridges and percussion caps, a battered telescope, and half-a-dozen half-empty bottles of tequila. The third wall boasted eight-foot arched double doors with glass panes looking out onto a veranda. The panes had been imported from the East.

Speck hissed and nodded to the open doorway in the fourth wall.

Clint pointed to his own chest, then at the door, indicating Speck was to remain behind. Staying in the shadows on the perimeter of the room, Clint ghosted to the open doorway, finding a hallway lined with benches on either side. Four doors, two on either side, opened off the hall, at the end of which, a flight of stairs led up to the second floor.

He pressed up against the wall when he heard stirring

behind one of the doors, his gun raised over his head to use as a club. After a moment, the noise subsided. Clint relaxed and crept to the end of the hall. He paused at the base of the stairs, then silently mounted them.

There were another half-dozen rooms off the hall, also lined with benches. Moving slowly Clint put his ear to each door, picking up enough movement to guess that each room had one or two hardcases in it. Satisfied, he started back to the stairs, but the door nearest the stairs creaked open and a pale, flickering light pushed away the early morning shadows.

Quickly, he dropped to his belly and scooted into the shadows under a bench just as a bearded cowboy in longjohns with a coal-oil lamp in one hand and a six-gun in the other stepped into the hall. Clint's blood ran cold when he recognized Pete Bodine.

A guttural voice called out from inside the room. "What's eatin' you now, Pete?"

"Thought I heard something," he growled, holding the lamp over his head.

"Probably one of them blasted rats running around here. They ain't going to bother you."

For another few seconds, Pete stood motionless. Then with a shrug of his shoulders, turned back into his room. As soon as the door closed, Clint slipped out, figuring the scuffling Bodine would make climbing back into his bunk would cover the faint sounds of Clint's boots on the heavy puncheon floor.

Moments later, Clint slipped back into the salon. At least, now, he had a better idea of the numbers they faced.

Quickly, he pulled out the stick of dynamite, cut it in two. He didn't want to blow the *hacienda* to pieces, just create enough damage to put some of Rawlings' hard-cases to thinking.

The first stick, he placed under the cold ashes in the living room fireplace, and the other, he stacked among the kindling logs in the second fireplace in the *cocina*, figuring when the fire was built later that morning, it would detonate the explosives.

"That ought to stir up some excitement," he whispered.

Speck chuckled. "Maybe give some of them old boys something to think about too."

"By the way. Our friends are here."

Speck frowned.

"The Bodine brothers."

Speck's eyes grew wide, then a grin played over his lips. "They're mighty stubborn *hombres*."

"They are that," Clint said, heading down the stairs into the storeroom where he paused to dig out two cured hams from a barrel, then hurried after Speck who was lugging the case of dynamite down the stairs into the tunnel. When Speck saw the hams, he lifted an eyebrow.

Chuckling, Clint stuck them in his saddlebags. "I've been hungry for a good ham."

Speck grinned. "Tired of my rabbit, huh?"

"Like they say, Partner—variety is the spice of life."

By the time they reached the cave high on the southern slope, the first gray of false dawn was slipping over the eastern ridges. Clint tended their ponies while Speck built up the banked fire. As they settled around the cheery blaze, the first explosion erupted, its thunder rolling across the snowy meadows as black and white smoke billowed into the clear sky.

"There's the first one," Clint remarked with a chuckle, slicing off thick slabs of ham and popping them in the heated skillet. On a flat rock propped up by the edge of the fire, corn cakes the size of silver dollars baked.

From their altitude on the mountain slope, they could see almost three quarters of the interior of the stockade-enclosed yard surrounding the *hacienda*. Several cowpokes were scurrying around, and even at this distance, the frightened squeals of horses carried to them on the crisp, cold air.

Moments later, a second explosion reverberated across the mountain slopes. This time, a ball of fire blasted into the sky, followed by a thick balloon of churning smoke.

Zeke Turner had just rolled out of his bunk when the first explosion rocked the *hacienda*.

"What the Sam Hill," he muttered, yanking his trousers on over his longjohns and grabbing his gunbelt as he bolted from the room.

Smoke filled the salon. Zeke slid to a halt and blinked against the thick pall of dust. Several chairs were overturned. Two cowpokes lay sprawled on the floor and two others staggered around, coughing and digging their balled fists in their eyes.

The adobe fireplace was demolished, leaving a hole

the size of a washtub in the outside wall through which cold air whistled.

Pete, followed by his brothers, stumbled into the room. "What's going on in here?"

Zeke jerked around from where he had been berating the Mexican *cocineros*. "I can't get nothing out of these women cooks except that when they started the fire in the kitchen, the fireplace blew up. Where in the blazes is Chochiti?"

By now, the icy wind blasting through the holes in the walls of the *hacienda* had cleared most of the smoke, leaving a thick layer of dust over the room and its furnishings.

Zeke barked commands at the cowering peons, sending them scurrying to plug the holes in the walls. Seconds later, a trembling peon hurried into the salon. "*Si, el Patron*. You wish for Chochiti?"

Zeke glared down at the cowering Mexican. "What's going on here, Chochiti? Who did all this?"

The trembling peon shook his head. "*Por favor*, *el Patron*. I do not know."

"Don't lie to me, you little—" He drew his arm back.

Ducking his head and whining, Chochiti dropped to his knees. "I do not lie, *el Patron*. Chochiti, he is teller of the truth, *por todo que es santo*, by all that is holy."

Turner sneered, then aimed a kick at the cowering peon. "Then get out of here. And find out who done it, understand?"

Later, around a table with platters of fried venison

and pots of steaming coffee, Pete glared at Zeke. "So, what caused the explosion? Any idea who done it?"

Zeke shook his head thoughtfully, then studied Bodine. His eyes grew cold. "Front and back gates closed and barred from inside. Same with the stable door. No one's come in or gone out. That means, whoever done it, is right here with us." He paused and glanced at a handful of hardcases standing behind the Bodines. "You and your brothers is the only ones new here." His tone was accusatory.

Beside Pete, Al stiffened. Pete glanced from the corner of his eye, seeing the hardcases behind them. He grinned easily at Zeke. "Reckon I was in your boots, I'd figure the same way. But, what reason we got? Me and my brothers come here to do a job for the sheriff. He paid us good. I figure on doing the job. I got nothing to gain by stirring up trouble with you old boys."

Pursing his lips, Zeke studied the bearded cowpoke staring at him from across the table. There was a look in Bodine's black eyes that sent a chill down his spine. "Just who is this Bowles hombre you're looking for?"

Pete told him, then asked, "What do you know about this Cooper hombre, the one Sheriff Faber wants dead?"

Zeke shook his head. "Nothing except we ain't been able to run him down. Him and those greaser *vaqueros* he runs with is slicker than calf slobber."

"What's Bowles to Cooper? Why would he want to come all the way up here from Tucson to help the hombre? What's he got to gain?"

Zeke shrugged. "Got no idea. Don't really care as long as we put the old man six feet under."

Pete toyed with the cup of coffee in his hand. "What's this Cooper done to the Sheriff that he wants to bury him?"

Zeke gulped down the rest of his coffee and gave Bodine a conspiratorial look. "Sheriff Faber and them he works for is taking over the country around here. This old coot didn't want to sell, so the sheriff run him out."

Pete studied Zeke. He leaned back. "Must be mighty valuable spread," he muttered, at the same time gazing idly around the room and remembering the noise that had awakened him earlier that morning.

Studying the ring of hard, cruel faces around them, Bodine couldn't believe any of them responsible. No, whoever placed the explosives had to come from outside, which meant there had to been a hidden entrance in the walls of the compound. For a moment, he considered sharing his little theory with Zeke, but decided against it until he had hard proof.

"Reckon it is, but it ain't none of my business or your business. The pay's good, so I do what I'm told. And that's what you do."

Suddenly, the door burst open and an excited cowboy bundled in a heavy coat rushed in. "Zeke! Red and Big Nose George is gone."

Zeke stared up at the excited cowboy in confusion. "What?"

Nodding emphatically, the cowpoke blurted out what he had discovered. "Me and Muleskinner went up to relieve them this morning. When we got to the cabin, they was gone. The cabin door was open, and it was all tore up inside." He paused and wrinkled his nose. "I don't know if it was a wolverine or badger or what, but some animal got in there and sprayed his stink all over the place. Rank enough to gag a dog on a gut wagon."

"To blazes with that," Zeke exclaimed jumping to his feet. "What happened to Red and Big Nose George?"

He shook his head. "I don't know. There was blood on the ground in front of the cabin. I left Muleskinner up there while I come back to tell you." He paused and glanced around the room, spotting the destroyed fireplace. Puzzled, he asked, "What happened here?"

One of the hardcases replied. "Something blew up. We don't know what."

The cowpoke looked back at Zeke. "Them must have been the explosions we heard up at the cabin. Didn't know what they were, though."

Zeke snapped, "Shut up. I got to think." After a moment, he gestured to the cowboy. "Bones, get on back there with Muleskinner. We'll take care of things here."

After Bones left, Zeke turned to another hardcase ranny. "Barker, you're our best tracker. You and Carson find out what happened to Big Nose George and Red."

Sitting at the heavy oak table in front of the fire, Pete poured another cup of coffee, trying to make sense of the night's events. The more he studied the explosions, the more convinced he became that the jasper who pulled it off was not among the Mexican servants or

Zeke's renegades. The hired guns had nothing to gain, and the Mexicans didn't have the guts. No, somehow, Clint Bowles had a hand in the night's events, but how, and why?

Chapter Sixteen

Back in the cave, Clint and Speck put themselves around a skillet of fried ham, corn cakes, and coffee thick enough to float a six-shooter, after which they rolled out their soogans for a well-deserved *siesta*.

The freckle-faced cowpoke lay staring at the rocky ceiling above. After a moment, he spoke up. "You know, Clint, I ain't never been a nosy jasper, but I can't help wondering just why old Sam didn't want to give us a hand. It don't make no sense to me. Do it to you?"

Clint remembered Maria's explanation. He didn't know if he believed her or not, but he understood what she meant for he had first hand experience living with the guilt for another's death. Now, by a stroke of good fortune, he no longer had to live with that guilt, and he would go to considerable lengths to avoid such an experience again.

127

"I'm not sure, Speck, but I reckon he just don't want it on his conscience should something happen to us."

Speck pondered the answer several moments. "Reckon I see what you mean, especially if it's a youngster you raised. I reckon that's why he sent Luiz after Miss Maria. But if something does happen, ain't he still going to have that same feeling because we was trying to help him out of a bind?"

Clint chuckled, and with a wry edge to his voice, grunted, "I reckon he'll have to work through that if the time comes."

Throughout the day, activity buzzed in the *hacienda* as the Mexican laborers struggled to repair the walls before dark. While a dozen swarmed the outside wall like ants, another dozen rebuilt the fireplace.

Several small bands of angry hardcases wandered the valley, probing into the foothills. Twice, voices carried up the slope, but the entrance of the arroyo leading up to the cave was hidden by the thick growth of white fir.

While the other hired guns rode out, Pete and his brothers remained behind, inspecting the walls surrounding the *hacienda*. "There ain't no way anyone can get through these walls except by them gates in front and back, Pete," Al remarked, his breath frosty in the icy air.

"What about the gate in the stable?"

Joe shrugged. "It was barred from inside. Only way a jasper could have gone out was for someone in here to lock it back."

Reluctantly, the older brother agreed, but he was still convinced that those responsible for the explosions did not come from inside the *hacienda*. On the other hand, he did not completely discard the idea of inside aid.

At the same time in a cantina fifteen miles south of the valley, Barker and Carson listened as Big Nose George, his words slurred with rotgut whiskey, told them what happened back at the cabin. "That jasper was faster than any gunnie I've ever seen." The middle-aged gunhand pointed to his eyes. "And I've seen the fast ones. Why, Red didn't even clear leather before his right shoulder was busted up. He's in a room upstairs drunker'n a skunk if you want to ask him."

"You recognize the shooter?"

"He was all bundled up in a heavy coat and wore a beard. I couldn't see anything else. Maybe Red saw him better. You want to go up and see him?"

Barker declined and headed back to the *hacienda*.

Two guards were camped in the corral beside the south guard cabin when Barker and Carson rode up. The cabin door and windows were wide open, but the rank stench of animal stink enveloped the small lodging. One of the gunman looked up at Barker. "I ain't getting paid enough to freeze my tail off out here. Either Zeke gets us another cabin, or I'm drawing my time."

Another mile down the twisting road, Barker reined up and stared at Carson. He wrinkled his nose. "You smell woodsmoke?"

Carson sniffed, then shrugged it off. "Probably the ranch. Wind's out of the north."

Barker nodded, but at that moment, his sharp eyes spotted a scar on a slab of gray granite by the side of the road, a scar that could have been made only by a horseshoe. His eyes scanned the slope above the road. A few feet higher, the ground was torn by a hoof.

Slowly, he surveyed the slope rising steeply above them, the pines so thick that someone could be watching fifty feet away and still be invisible from the road.

Far up on a slope overlooking the road, Clint frowned as the two riders stared at the side of the road where he had climbed out the day before after sending Red and Big Nose George on their way.

He held his breath when the dark-skinned cowpoke looked up. After a few moments, they rode on, and Clint sighed with relief.

He watched until they disappeared down the road, and then turned back to the new cave he had just discovered. It was near the crest of the ridge where the towering pines and firs didn't block the sun, a perfect sunning spot for rattlesnakes on warm days.

Dismounting, he pulled a lighter pine torch and a heavy canvas bag from his saddlebags and headed into the cave. More than once as a youth with the Comanche, he and the other Comanche boys searched the deep confines of caves in the winter and pulled out lethargic snakes that made for right tasty meals.

Thirty minutes later, Clint emerged with a canvas

sack heavy with half-a-dozen sluggish rattlesnakes. A crooked grin played over his bearded face as he imagined the reaction of the hardcases back at the *hacienda*.

The Bodines and several grizzled cowpokes looked on as Barker told Zeke what he had learned. "The jasper was a complete stranger. George had never seen him. He said the old boy was fast. Faster than he'd ever seen. He just rode up and told them to light a shuck out of there."

"He say what the jasper looked like."

Barker shrugged. "All he said was he had a beard."

Pete shot a look at his brothers and nodded. They grinned back at him. It was Bowles.

"A beard? That's all he saw?"

"That's all," Barker replied. "But, I found something we might ought to take a look at. On the way back from the cabin, I run across where a single horse left the road and climbed the mountain slope."

Zeke studied him a moment. "Fresh?"

"A day. Not much more. Could be that bearded hombre." He paused, then cautioned, "And it could be just a wandering Injun. I reckon there's still a few Navahos from Bosque Redondo drifting around out there."

"Well, let's go see," Zeke replied, pushing to his feet.

Barker shook his head. "Too late today. We can go in the morning. Leave early and get there by first light."

Upstairs in their room, the Bodines discussed the news about the bearded gunman. "It's Bowles," Pete growled, reaching for his bag of Bull Durham. "Got to be. For whatever reason, he come up here to give this Cooper hombre a hand."

Joe glanced at Al. "So what you got in mind, Pete? You want us to ride out with them old boys in the morning or go it on our own?"

Pete spread tobacco in the curl of paper in his hand. "Let's don't worry about the morning." He glanced up with a sly look on his face. "I figure maybe we ought to take care of tonight first."

Al and Joe exchanged puzzled looks. "What do you mean by that, Pete?" Al asked, reaching for the Bull Durham.

"Just this." He paused to roll the cigarette and run the tip of his tongue along the paper and gently fold it over with his fingers. He twisted the ends and looked up. "Stop and think. Bowles come up here to help this Cooper hombre. Now, there's got to be a good reason for a jasper to ride all the way from Tucson. Maybe them two is kin. I don't know, but it's something important. Now, this here *hacienda* belonged to Cooper. For all we know, Bowles might have lived here a spell with the old man. Shoot fire, he mighta helped him build the place. Whatever it was, it stands to reason he could know all the tricks of getting in or out of here without nobody seeing nothing, don't it?"

Al frowned for a moment, then his grizzled face lit with understanding. "Yeah. I see what you're getting at."

"Me too," Joe exclaimed. He hesitated and then frowned. "So, what does that all mean?"

Pete rolled his eyes. "It means that the three of us is

going to keep a sharp eye out tonight just in case we get us another midnight visitor."

Joe's frown deepened. "You think he'd be dumb enough to come back tonight?"

Taking a deep breath, Pete studied his youngest brother. For some reason, Little Joe was never real bright. He'd never been kicked by a horse, or their ma hadn't dropped him on his head, but he had always been a tad slower than a snail on a greased log. "He wants to run us off from this here *hacienda*. He figures he causes enough headaches, Zeke and his old boys will pull out. So, I figure he's coming back tonight and bring some more headaches with him." He paused and studied his two brothers. "Now, you understand?"

Little Joe's brows knit in confusion, but he nodded his head eagerly. "Yeah. I understand, Pete. I understand real good."

Around the small fire in the cave during a supper of ham, corn cakes, and coffee, Speck leaned back against the wall of the cave and said, "We got away sneaking in the *hacienda* last night because them old boys wasn't expecting nothing. But, they'll be watching tonight, Clint. I guarantee you."

Chuckling, Clint replied. "That's what I'm counting on except, they'll be watching the wrong place."

Speck frowned. "Wrong place?"

"Yep." Clint nodded to a stack of fused dynamite sticks. "I made those for you. After I leave, you ride out in the valley about a mile from the *hacienda*—give me a hour, then set off those sticks of dynamite one at a time in different spots about a quarter mile apart. It'll draw the attention of every hardcase at the ranch. While they're watching the fireworks, I'll take care of everything else." He nodded to the securely tied bag of rattlesnakes lying in the cold wind just outside the mouth of the cave. The icy weather would keep the deadly serpents in their somnolent state until he turned them loose.

And then the warmth of the *hacienda* would do its job.

Pete waited until the entire house was bedded down before rousing his brothers. "Joe, I want you at the door in the kitchen. From there you can keep an eye on the back gate. Al, you take the front doors and watch the front gate. Me, I'll find a dark corner in the salon downstairs. If he comes in, he's got to sneak through the salon."

The three brothers grinned at each other.

Pete added with a cruel grin. "You see any jasper skulking about, shoot."

Speck gently packed the dynamite into his saddlebags which he had stuffed with pine needles to cushion the oily sticks. Tying the bags to the cantle of his saddle, he glanced over the back of his yellow dun at Clint. "You got until the handle of the dipper points west," he announced, referring to the Big Dipper in the northern skies.

Clint gave the cinch a final tug and tightened the tip

of the leather strap under an O-ring. "I'll be ready." He checked his saddlebag and the four sticks of dynamite, then picked up the bag of rattlesnakes and the forked-branch he had cut and swung into the saddle. While the chilling cold acted like a numbing drug on the rattlesnakes, the jarring ride would stimulate them, and then when the warmth of the *hacienda* heated their blood, they would become active enough to catch the attention of even the orneriest owlhoot.

Speck swung into his saddle. "You be careful, Clint." He rubbed the back of his neck. "I got a bad feeling they'll be looking for you."

Chapter Seventeen

Forty-five minutes later, Clint paused at the closed door at the top of the stairs to the *cocina*. He listened intently for the slightest sound in the kitchen, but the dark house breathed silently. From time to time down below came the squeak of a mouse, or the scratch of rat's feet scrabbling across the floor.

The bag in his hand jerked. The rattlesnakes were becoming active.

Minutes dragged. From the salon, the Regulator clock struck one. Growing impatient, Clint slowly lifted the locking bar on the door.

Across the room, Joe had been peering through a gunport in a window shutter when he heard the scratch of wood on wood. By now, his eyes had grown accustomed to the dark and some shadows stood out more distinctly than others.

136

He scooted around in his chair. The legs scraped on the tile floor.

Behind the door, Clint froze, peering through the crack in the direction of the noise. He squinted his eyes in an effort to discern shapes from shadows. And then, a shadow moved. He held his breath. The shadow floated in his direction. Silently shucking his six–gun, he cursed his impatience for not waiting until the first explosion.

To his relief, a muffled explosion rumbled through the *hacienda*, followed by hushed exclamations. Footsteps on the flagstone floor rushed past the closed door. Quickly, Clint slipped out and ducked into the shadows of the ponderous table in the middle of the kitchen.

The explosions continued, one about every six or seven minutes. By now, voices echoed throughout the *hacienda* as cowboys scrambled upstairs to the second floor balconies.

Moving quickly, Clint ducked into the hallway and dumped the snakes on the floor.

Still lethargic, they offered little resistance as he used the forked-branch to toss one through each of the open doorways. He had two left. He cut his eyes upward toward the Bodines' room.

Outside, the explosions continued. Excited curses came from above. Quickly picking up one of the rattlers, Clint hurried upstairs, keeping his eyes on the bedroom doors opening to the balcony. The thick-bodied rattler started to writhe and squirm on the forked-branch.

At the top of the stairs, he crouched behind the railing and eased forward until he could toss the rattler through the open door into Bodine's room, then hurried back down.

He skidded to a halt in the middle of the hall. The last rattlesnake had disappeared. Clint gulped, then keeping his eyes on the shadows at his feet, hurried through the salon and *cocina*.

Just as he stepped into the kitchen, a terrified scream ripped apart the silence followed by a barrage of gunfire. Clint jerked open the door to the stairway, then hesitated. Quickly, he crossed the room and threw open the back door as a blind trail, then hurried back down into the storeroom.

Clint rode hard, bypassing the cave and climbing the mountain until he reined up on a granite outcropping across the south road and high above the sentries' cabin as false dawn grayed the sky. The cabin door re- mained open, and a small fire burned in the corral where the two guards had taken shelter in the stable.

Fumbling in his saddlebags, Clint fished out the four cut sticks of dynamite. Lighting a match, he touched the flame to the fuses and one by one, lobbed them over the edge of the outcropping down on the cabin and cor- ral below.

At the first explosion, the horses bolted. The second explosion sent the hardcases jumping for cover. After the fourth explosion, they were scrambling up the road after their stampeding horses.

The *hacienda* was in turmoil. Five rattlesnakes had been killed; two hardcases accidentally wounded from frantically thrown shots; and three more were in the midst of packing their gear and riding out.

"I didn't ask for no rattlesnakes," one exclaimed as he threw his bedroll over his shoulder and stalked from the *hacienda*.

Barker stood in the middle of the salon watching Zeke storm back and forth. "Counting Red and Big Nose George, that's the fifth jasper to leave. And we got two shot up bad enough they got to get to the doctor back in El Jardin. That leaves us an even dozen."

"Fifteen, counting me and my brothers," Pete put in.

Turner glanced at Bodine, then spun on Barker, his face twisted with rage. "Saddle up your ponies. We're riding out and we're going to string up that bearded cuss who's behind all this." He paused, then fixed Bodine with a hard look. "All fifteen of us. And five double eagles to him what brings the jasper in."

At that moment, the grumble of four faint explosions rumbled through the air. Barker frowned at Zeke. "Now what it the Sam Hill was that?"

Bodine arched an eyebrow. He didn't know what the explosions were, but he knew who was behind them.

Back at the cave, Clint swung down and ground reined his gray. Speck looked up from the fire. "Any problems?"

"Nope." Clint shook his head. "But, I figure we best find us another spot."

With a crooked grin, Speck looked around the cave. "And just when I was beginning to call this place home."

Thirty minutes later on a steep slope overlooking the south road, Clint reined up in a dense stand of white fir and lodgepole pine. "Like I figured. We got visitors."

Speck followed the direction of Clint's gaze. In the middle of the valley, over a dozen riders were pounding hard toward the south road. "Hey, ain't that Bodine up front?"

Clint narrowed his eyes. "Looks like it." He chuckled. "Kind of early for them fellers to be out. They must not have got themselves much sleep."

"Reckon not."

They remained motionless in the thick forest as the band of riders drew nearer. The rhythmic pounding of hooves reached their ears, and the sound intensified as the riders raced past some two hundred yards below.

After the hoofbeats died out, Clint clicked his tongue and his gray picked its way down the slope and across the road into the forest beyond. The first creek they reached, he led them upstream, coming out on a bed of rocks. Several feet up the bank, they reached a shale outcropping. Clint reined up, returned to the bed, and righted what few rocks turned up by the ponies' hooves. He grinned up at Speck. "I don't figure they'll pay much attention to sign in the road, but we best lay a couple blind trails just in case."

Zeke cursed when he saw the demolished cabin and corral. And he cursed louder when he saw the boot-prints of Bones and Muleskinner heading south along the muddy road.

Barker arched an eyebrow and with a wry grin, re-marked. "That's two more, Zeke."

Zeke glared at the grinning cowboy with a murder-ous rage. "Go to hades." The infuriated ramrod di-vided his men, sending each of the four groups in different directions with a promise of a sizeable bonus for whichever band of riders brought the bearded cowpoke in. "Search every inch of them woods. I want that bearded no-account." He turned to Ace. "Now, show me them scar marks. We'll follow that trail."

By noon, Zeke and his small band had combed over two miles of the southern foothills facing the *hacienda* when they rode upon the cave Clint and Speck had left behind that morning.

"From the looks of sign, there was more than just that bearded jasper," Barker said, squatting on the floor of the cave. "I figure he's got hisself a sidekick."

Zeke turned his eyes back on the valley below. "That was the one setting of them explosions last night while our man dumped off that pile of rattlesnakes." A hard, cruel killer, Zeke could still appreciate the cleverness of the bearded hombre. That was the kind of hombre Zeke wouldn't mind have working for him.

Barker swung back in the saddle and surveyed the forest about them. "Well, boss. I don't know where he is, but he ain't around here. Maybe he's hightailed it out of this part of the country."

Zeke shook his head. "Not likely. Not likely."

"This looks like a good spot to hole up in," Clint muttered as they emerged from a stand of golden-leafed aspen and came upon a granite overhang. "Trees in front and a way out in the back," he noted, nodding to the canyon behind the ledge. He glanced over his shoulder at the valley spreading out two hundred feet below. "And a clear view of both roads coming into the valley."

While Speck set about building a smokeless fire, Clint picked his way down the slope to the stream below to fill the canteens. Popping the cork back in the last one, he started back up the slope when he heard horses. He slipped behind the thick bole of an ancient pine and peered in the direction of their camp.

Moments later, a guttural voice rolled down the slope. "Hold it right there, hombre."

Clint studied the pine and fir on the slope above him, but could see no one. A second voice spoke. "Put up them hands and don't move a muscle."

Speck's unnaturally loud voice drifted down to Clint. "Who are you? What do you want? I ain't done nothing."

Silently, Clint laid the canteens on the ground and eased around the side of the slope to come up from behind. As the camp came into sight, he saw three cow-pokes on the ground, holding six-guns on Speck. A wide sneer on his face, the fourth leaned forward in his saddle, hands folded on the saddle horn.

One of the hombres on the ground disarmed Speck and slipped the six-gun under his belt. He nodded to Clint's gray. "Where's the jasper what belongs to this animal?" he asked, holstering his side arm.

The other two holstered their six-guns now that Speck was disarmed. "Yeah," one growled, taking a threatening step forward. "You best tell us, or we'll beat it out of you." He tapped his fist into the palm of his other hand. "And you won't like that."

Clint groaned with resignation. He'd killed enough people in his life. So far, no one had died at his hands in the valley. He hoped none would, but that, he knew, would depend on them.

He stepped from behind a pine. His cold voice carried across the clearing. "You ain't going to beat anybody, friend."

As one, the four hardcases jerked around.

Clint faced them coolly, his eyes cold, his muscles relaxed, his arms hanging loosely at his side. His gray eyes searched the faces of the four for a hint of what action they would take. "Smartest move you jaspers could make is fork them ponies and ride out of the valley. There's nothing waiting here for you except a heap of misery."

A narrow-shouldered cowpoke, shorter than the others, stepped forward. He wore fur chaps and a gray plaid wool coat. "Well, boys. Take a look. Here's the jasper Zeke's looking for. He's worth five double eagles." He held his hands out to his side, flexing his fingers.

"Yeah." The one who had taken Speck's six-gun grinned and stepped to the side for a clear shot at Clint.

"You boys are making a mistake." The warning in Clint's tone was obvious.

The owlhoot in the saddle frowned, then glanced down at his partners, addressing the one in the gray plaid coat. "Listen, Shorty. Remember what Big Nose George told Ace. If this hombre is the one, he's fast, real fast."

Shorty kept his eyes on Clint. From the side of his lips, he hissed, "Shut up, Dink. I ain't never met no one I couldn't take."

One of the gunnies to his side chuckled. "Take the pilgrim, Shorty. He don't look so tough."

Shorty flexed the fingers of his hand hovering above the butt of his six-gun. His eyes narrowed. "One way or another, cowboy, I'm taking you and your partner there back to the ranch."

The gunmen on either side of Shorty grinned, hunching their shoulders and bending their arms. Their fingers hovered over the butts of their six-guns.

Clint drawled, "You might be going back, but not with me."

Shorty's face twisted in anger. "We'll see about that," he shouted.

All three gunnies grabbed for their six-guns at the same time.

Chapter Eighteen

The twin .36 Colts leaped into Clint's hands, belching yellow spurts of fire. Half-a-dozen booming gunshots blurred together, and a cloud of gray smoke billowed up obliterating the scene.

When the north breeze blew away the smoke, three gunslingers lay sprawled on the ground, one unmoving with his fingers wrapped about the butt of the sidearm still in the holster, and the other two writhing about on the muddy ground, one clutching his belly, the other his shoulder.

Clint turned the .36s on the young man in the saddle.

Dink threw up his hands. "Not me, Mister. I ain't stupid."

Indicating the fallen owlhoots, Clint growled, "Throw them on their horses and get them out of here. You tell your boss, Zeke, if he don't pack up his warbags and light a shuck out of this valley, him and every jasper down there will be a free meal for the coyotes."

The young gunhand gulped and nodded jerkily. His face paled. "Yes, sir. I will. I sure will."

Before Dink was a hundred yards from the camp, the gutshot gunhand joined Shorty on that rickety ladder down to hades.

As soon as Dink and his grisly load vanished into he forest, Clint and Speck moved their camp.

An hour later, Dink pulled up at the stable and dismounted. He glanced toward the *hacienda* and spotted two Mexican peons carrying out the limp body of Barker. Behind them came Carson, Barker's sidekick, carrying a dead rattlesnake.

Dink frowned at the rattler. "What the blazes happened to Ace, Burk?"

Burk grunted, his gray grizzled beard catching the last of the winter sun. "Snakebite. I don't reckon we found all the rattlers that jasper turned loose in the house. Old Ace there poured hisself a stiff drink to chase off the cold of the day's ride. He plopped hisself down on a bench by the fireplace and that blasted snake came out of one of them jars underneath," He whirled the headless serpent over his head and slung it over the wall. "The boys done tore the house apart for others. Didn't find none, but that don't mean they ain't there." He glanced fearfully back at the *hacienda*. "I don't cotton to sleeping in there tonight. Too many hidey-holes for them snakes."

Dink gulped, looking at the two dead cowpokes

draped over their saddles and the body of Barker being carried into the stable. Right now, he told himself, cutting his eyes back toward the open gate in the stone stockade surrounding the *hacienda,* those wide-open spaces looked mighty appealing. He drew a deep breath. "Reckon I'd best see Zeke. Let him know what happened out there."

In the salon where Zeke was slouched over the heavy table, Dink related the events of the afternoon. Several gunhands, including the Bodines, stood around, eyes narrowed, jaws set, listening intently.

Zeke jumped to his feet. "Shorty? He got Shorty?"

The slender hired gun nodded. "Shorty never cleared leather." He nodded to a young cowpoke in the kitchen being tended by a Mexican woman and her daughter. "Then the jasper busted Arkansas' shoulder and put a lead plum in Blacky's belly. Blacky died on the way back. He's out in the stable with Shorty."

"And Ace," Zeke added.

Dink shook his head in amazement. "I never saw the jasper's hands move, Zeke. One second they were at his side, and before I could blink them Colts was in his hands." He shook his head. "It was like some kind of Injun magic."

Fire blazed from Zeke's eyes. He grabbed the bottle of tequila and turned it up, gulping the last few swallows of the fiery liquid. He slammed it to the table. "Chochiti. Bring me another bottle. *Pronto!*" he cursed loudly. Under a three-day-old beard, his clenched jaw writhed like a nest of snakes. His black eyes glittered.

"So he thinks he's going to make us all into coyote bait, huh?" He slapped his sidearm. "Well, that dumb jasper has got hisself another think coming. He can't outgun us all."

The slender outlaw shot a nervous glance at Carson. He licked his lips. "I'm telling you, Zeke, that hombre is faster than a cut cat. I ain't never seen nobody that fast."

Zeke snorted.

Chochiti scurried in with another bottle. Zeke grabbed it and yanked the cork loose. He turned it up and took several gulps.

Pete stepped forward. All eyes in the salon turned on him as he spoke to Dink. "This bearded gent. He have a partner, a freckle-faced fencepost?"

Dink nodded, his eyes momentarily widening in surprise.

Bodine looked at Zeke. "That's Clint Bowles, the jasper I'm after." He frowned at Dink. "If I'd of been with you old boys, Bowles would be dead now." He hesitated, debating as to whether he should lay out his theory about Bowles to Zeke, then decided he had nothing to gain by keeping it to himself.

He pulled up a chair across the table from Zeke. "This Bowles jasper has some connection with Cooper, the old man who owned this spread. I don't got no idea what it is, but it's mighty important to him."

Zeke frowned.

Bodine continued, "He's come all the way from Tucson, so it's got to be important. Don't it seem like that to you?"

The burly ramrod pondered the question, then nodded slowly. "Go on."

Pausing to pour himself a drink from Zeke's bottle, Pete sneered. "I tried to talk to some of these greasers about the old man—see if there be some connection between them, but them Mexicans—they *no hablo* English soon as I bring up the Sam Cooper who build this place."

The diminutive peon, Chochiti, sidled over to Zeke and whispered in his ear. The outlaw cut his eyes toward the kitchen, and a sly grin twisted his rocky face.

Carson spotted the grin on Zeke's face. "What you got in mind, Zeke? Counting Ace and them two out there, we're down to twelve."

Dink nodded to the cowpoke being tended by one of the Mexican women. "Eleven. Arkansas over there's got his shoulder busted up. That woman and her daughter can't tend him proper-like. He's got to have a doctor set his bones."

Zeke poured another drink of tequila and downed it hastily. He drew the back of his rough hand over his lips and eyes narrowed. He slapped his glass down on the table.

In the kitchen, *Señora* Inez and her daughter, Damita, wrapped a bandage about Arkansas' shoulder, deliberately ignoring the sudden noise.

Zeke barked, "*Oye! La chica! La chica!*" *Señora* Inez glanced around when he called her daughter. Zeke jabbed a thick finger at the girl. "*Poco chica! Viene aquí, pronto.* Little girl, come here, fast."

Muttering softly in her daughter's ear, the fearful

señora gently urged her daughter into the salon. Zeke grinned cruelly and spoke to the mother. "*Señora.* You speak English?"

She shook her head slowly. Zeke grunted and pulled his six-gun and put it to the frightened girl's head. "*Señ*ora! English?"

Señora Inez's face froze in horror. She clasped her hands and fell to her knees. "*Si, Señor.* I speak English."

He motioned her to him with the muzzle of his six-gun. "How long you live here, *Señora*? At the *hacienda*?"

Her eyes were wide with fear. She laid her hand on her whimpering daughter's arm. "Many years, *Señor.* Please. We have done nothing."

Leaning forward in his chair, Zeke grunted. "Tell me what I want to know, and nothing will happen to you. *Comprende*?"

She nodded. "*Si, si.* I tell you what you ask." She shot a murderous look at Chochiti, who dropped his eyes submissively.

Zeke grinned up at Carson, then glared at the frightened woman. "The old man who lived here, Sam Cooper. You know him?"

She nodded eagerly.

"He have any family?"

"*Si. Una esposa y la hija.* A wife and daughter. His wife, *la esposa*, she is dead."

A puzzled frown wrinkled Zeke's forehead. "That's all?"

In halting English, she said. "A son, but he too is dead."

Pete spoke up. "What was his name?" He glanced at Zeke, fully expecting to hear the words, Clint Bowles.

She hesitated.

Zeke narrowed his eyes and raised the muzzle of his six-gun to the young *señorita's* temple.

Her words gushed out. "He was called Cleve Bollinger."

The name rocked everyone in the room back on his heels.

Chapter Nineteen

Excited murmurs filled the room.

"Bollinger!" Bodine muttered.

"He's dead," Carson said. "Burned up in a fire down in Valverde eight or ten years ago."

"Yeah," one of the hardcases put in. "Figured out who he was by the ivory-handled six-gun they found at his side."

"He was fast," another said.

Zeke leaned forward, his bearded face only inches from the trembling Mexican woman. His breath stunk of tequila and his eyes blazed with hate. "Cooper have any other family?"

She shook her head emphatically. "No, *Señor.*" She made a sign of the cross on her breast. "No family."

Leaning back, Zeke released the child who rushed

into her mother's arms. He waved them away with his six-gun.

For several moments, he studied the dark, thick table in front of him, half-a-dozen random thoughts tumbling through his whiskey-soaked brain. Finally, he looked up at the hard faces watching him. "Who said Bollinger burned up?"

A cold-eyed hired-gun stepped forward. "That was me."

"How do you know Bollinger burned up, Willy?"

Sliding his Stetson to the back of his head, Willy Adams grinned, revealing several gaps in his yellow teeth. "I was there, Zeke." He glanced around at the eyes fixed on him and grinned, feeling a sense of importance. "Why, I even saw the body." He wrinkled his nose. "My old lady never could burn bacon that bad, but she tried."

The room chuckled.

A wild idea hit Zeke. He studied Willy. "Did you know Bollinger?"

"Nope." Willy shook his head. "Never saw him."

Zeke shot Pete an amused smile and turned back to Willy. "So, you don't know for certain that was Bollinger."

The middle-aged owlhoot glanced around the room, suddenly not feeling quite as important, then shrugged. "Not me. The sheriff said the gun was Bollinger's. So he figured the body was Bollinger. Must have been right," he added. "Cause I never heard of nobody ever laying an eyeball on Bollinger again."

Zeke's brain whirred with possibilities. He narrowed his eyes on Pete and nodded to the mountains beyond the *hacienda.* "What was the name of this old boy out there?"

Pete frowned, wondering what was on the grizzled ramrod's mind. "Clint Bowles."

"Clint Bowles, huh?" Zeke leaned back and stared at the wrought-iron lamp hanging from the huge beam overhead. After a few moments, he cut his eyes toward Bodine. "Anything strike you as funny?"

"Funny?"

"Yeah. Like a fluke–what someone might call a twist of fate."

Brows knit, Bodine shook his head slowly. "Like what?"

Zeke leaned forward and tapped his finger on the table. "First. Like this jasper out there is fast. Bollinger was fast." He tapped his finger again. "Second. This jasper come to help Cooper. If Bollinger was alive, he'd likely come help out his old man." He tapped his finger a third time. "And last, Cleve Bollinger is the same initials as Clint Bowles."

For several moments, Pete stared at Zeke, the puzzled frown on his grizzled face slowly turning into shocked disbelief. "You don't figure—"

Zeke chuckled. "Nothing else makes no sense. A stranger ain't going to take on a whole blasted army for some old man with a Mexican squaw and half breed whelp." He slammed the side of his fist down on the table, causing the glasses to jump. "That ain't Clint Bowles out there—it's Cleve Bollinger!"

He looked around and jabbed a thick finger at Dink. "Dink, you pack Arkansas on his horse and take him to El Jardin. Leave right now. Tell Hitch Faber he'd best send an army out here because him and Rawlings is going up against Cleve Bollinger! You hear?"

No sooner than Dink and Willy helped Arkansas from the kitchen where his wounds had been dressed, *Señora* Inez hurried her daughter to their cramped quarters where she hastily told her husband of the conversation.

The slight Mexican peon frowned at her in surprise. "*Señor* Cleve? But he is *muerto.*"

She shrugged and repeated what she had overhead. She shoved him toward the door. "Hear me, Diego. Find Jorge Castel. He must go. He must tell *el Patron* what we have learned."

He turned to leave, but she laid her hand on his shoulder. "Say nothing of this to Chochiti. He is not to be trusted."

Speck squatted by the small fire, cupping a hot tin mug of coffee in his hands, studying the valley and the *hacienda* through the stand of white-barked aspen. "I got to admit, Clint. Sam does have him a right pretty place here. You'd figure he'd be fighting back instead of hiding in them caves."

Clint grunted. "Like he said, he don't have the guns to fight back. Rawlings and them no-accounts like him, all they got to do is take it over and hold on to it. Them that's been run out into the cold either fights back or packs up and starts over somewhere else. That's what that bunch of jayhawkers and carpetbaggers are figuring on."

"Shame Sam's got no law to turn to."

A cruel twist curled Clint's lips. "One day, the law, the real law will come in. Until then—" He laid his hand on the butt of one of his Colts. "This is the only law that kind understands."

"Uh oh." Speck sat up. He nodded to the far side of the valley where two riders raced along the edge of the shadows of the setting sun. "Somebody's in a hurry. Two of them. Looks like the jaspers back up at the cave."

Clint watched silently. Suddenly, his eyes picked up a third horseman, this one closer to the river, perhaps half a mile beyond the first two, a Mexican from his size and dress. He pursed his lips, frowning.

"What do you reckon them two jaspers is up to?" Speck drawled.

A faint grin played over his thickly bearded face. Absently, he scratched at the scar on his cheek. "I reckon Zeke has figured the time's come to bring in some outside help."

Speck chuckled. "You reckon?"

"Yes, sir. I certainly do."

Behind them, the faint cry of a thrush broke the silence of the setting sun, a series of several pure notes, each rising to a crescendo, then fading away.

Speck jerked around, but Clint simply grinned to himself and held his arm over his head, motioning for the visitor to come in. "Welcome my friend," he called out over his shoulder.

Ojo Blanco suddenly appeared from the undergrowth behind the camp. Behind him were the young warriors, Strong Swimmer and Hair Rope.

Clint gestured to the small fire. "Come. Sit. There is food for your bellies and much sugar for your coffee," he said, knowing the Kiowa-Apaches' love for sugar.

While the young warriors ate ravenously, Ojo Blanco sipped his coffee and said, "We have looked on. Many men seek you."

Clint nodded and explained why he was being sought. "This land belongs to my father. He paid the Navaho chief, Ornate, much gold. Now the gringo wants it. They drive my father and his people from the ranch."

Ojo grinned wryly.

Clint nodded at the insinuation in the old warrior's eyes. He chuckled. "You're right, my friend. Just as the whites did the Indian." He tapped his chest with his fingers. "I will take the land back."

Shaking his head slowly, Ojo said, "Many have tried, but the white man is too strong. Maybe, Bowles, these white eyes are also too strong." With a chuckle, Clint reached for the coffee pot and poured himself another cup. The old Apache warrior extended his cup, and Clint refilled it. "They are many, Bowles. But we will help."

The two young warriors glanced at each other. One arched an eyebrow, but neither uttered a word. Ojo Blanco spoke rapidly in the Athapascan dialect. Both young braves nodded. Ojo gestured to one of the warriors. "Hair Rope will go now before the sun sets. He will bring others."

The young warrior looked up. He cut his eyes toward Clint, then nodded. "I go."

Moments later, like a tenuous breath of air, the wiry warrior had vanished into the darkness beyond the flickering firelight.

The older Apache licked the grease from his fingers. He cocked his head at Clint. "What magic do you use for the great explosions?"

"No magic. It is a white man's invention," Clint replied, knowing that the old Apache could not be familiar with the new explosive. He pulled out a stick, put it in Ojo's hands, and explained its use.

Ojo nodded. "You have more?" His black eyes twinkled though his weathered face remained stoic.

With a wry grin, Clint handed him six sticks and demonstrated how to insert fuses.

Ojo grunted. "You have fire for fuses?"

Opening an oilcloth bag, Clint pulled out a handful of lucifers and handed them to the Apache.

"Good." Ojo pushed to his feet and nodded to Strong Swimmer. "We go."

After the two disappeared silently into the thick undergrowth behind the camp, Clint rolled out his soogan. He glanced up at the darkening sky. "A few clouds pushing in. Reckon it's going to be a mite cold tonight, partner. Better bundle up good and snug."

Speck frowned. "You going to sleep? It's still light."

Clint grinned. "Yep. Why? Don't you cotton to that notion?"

"Yeah, but I just figured you was going to figure some other way to stir up trouble down at the *hacienda*."

With a soft chuckle, Clint pulled the blankets up around his neck against the chilly air. "Believe me, partner. Unless I'm mistaken, Ojo Blanco is going to stir up a heap of trouble down there tonight. You best grab some snooze time while you can."

Speck raised up on one elbow. "What do you mean by that?"

Clint chuckled. "You'll see."

Deputy John Drucker reined up on a bluff overlooking a narrow trail below. A sneer played over his lips as he reached for his saddlegun. A solitary Apache rode the trail. Drucker's sneer broadened. Soon he would have another Apache scalp worth fifty dollars.

Hair Rope never heard the report of the Henry.

Clint stiffened as a single gunshot echoed through the mountains. His blood ran cold.

Chapter Twenty

Scattered dark clouds rushed past the waning moon, casting racing shadows across the snow-covered valley like a herd of stampeding mustangs, revealing from time to time a smaller, darker shadow ghosting toward the *hacienda*.

Without hesitation, the shadow scaled the wall and vanished.

Suddenly, a muffled explosion rolled across the valley.

Strong Swimmer crouched in the shadows of the stable, watching the *hacienda* as lights inside flickered aflame. Shadows rushed past the windows, heading for the upstairs balconies.

Staying in a crouch, the wiry young warrior dashed across the hardpan and into the *hacienda*. Moments later, he slipped back to the corral where he threw open the stable doors and stampeded the horses.

He swung up on the bare back of a frightened mare and lying low over her neck with his fingers intertwined in her mane, raced into the night.

Speck jerked upright. "What—"

Sleepily, Clint muttered. "Probably just Ojo playing with the dynamite. Go back to sleep."

Ignoring his partner, Speck leaped to his feet and peered out across the valley. With the moonlight reflecting off the snow, it was almost like daytime.

Suddenly, to the south down in the valley, an orange flame ballooned in the night followed by the thunder of exploding dynamite. The lanky cowpoke frowned, trying to figure out just what was going on.

The valley grew silent.

A few minutes later came another explosion, this one a half mile or so from the previous. Minutes passed, and then another echoed off the mountain slopes.

Then, without warning, a black hole appeared in the stockade wall surrounding the *hacienda* and shadows like a swarm of ants burst out, scattering across the valley. The squeal of frightened horses drifted across the snow.

Speck grinned. Now he knew why the old Apache warrior had wanted the dynamite. He crawled back into his bedroll.

"Satisfied?" Clint mumbled.

"Yeah. Real satisfied."

* * *

Infuriated curses erupted from the *hacienda* when the hardcases saw their ponies galloping madly across the valley.

Zeke clenched his fists and cursed as the shock of understanding hit him between the eyes like a singletree. He spun on his heel and raced downstairs and slid to a halt in the salon.

There, lying in the middle of the ponderous table was a three-foot arrow with three white feathers of the turkey vulture. Zeke's eyes grew wide. He grabbed the arrow, then looked around fearfully. "Search this place. There was an Injun here, an Apache!"

One of the hardcases protested. "What about the horses? They're scattering all over the valley."

The grizzled ramrod grimaced. "Blast! All right." He nodded to a hatchet-faced owlhoot. "Martin, you and Fuller get out there and round up what horses you can. The rest of you, tear this place apart, and look out for rattlers."

Ten minutes later, the small band of hardcases gathered back in the salon, having found no sign of the Apache or snakes. Willy shook his head. "Not a trace. How do you know it was Apache?"

Zeke set his jaw and glared at the middle-aged gunman. "This is how," he barked, tossing the arrow on the table. "No arrowhead, only a sharpened end." He touched a scarred finger to the feathers. "Three feathers instead of two. This is a war arrow." He sneered at Willy. "That's how I know."

Bodine grunted, "Reckon that explains the stampede."

Zeke arched an eyebrow. "Then why did that buck go to so much trouble to leave the arrow on the table. It's like he wanted us to know who took the horses."

In a burst of rage, he grabbed the arrow and snapped it into several pieces and slung them into the fireplace. He glared at his men. "We're going out in the morning, and we ain't coming back until we've put enough holes in this Clint Bowles or Cleve Bollinger or whoever in the Sam Hill he is." He glared around the room. "I'm upping the bonus on Bollinger. Two hundred dollars."

Sheriff Hitch Faber listened in disbelief as the young gun hand relayed Zeke Turner's message. "He's run off four and kilt three. Zeke's got hisself nine men left. Ten counting him. That's including them three Bodines you sent out there."

Behind the sheriff, Clatter Dowd glanced briefly at Deputy George Scruggs and muttered a curse. "Cleve Bollinger. No wonder that jasper looked familiar. It's been over ten years, but now that I got the name, the face fits. Older, heavier, and that beard covers it up, but Zeke's right, Sheriff. That was Cleve Bollinger."

Scruggs fleshy face paled. He gulped hard. "This means trouble, Hitch. Bad trouble."

Faber spun on the whining deputy. His eyes blazed. "Stop the sniveling." He rolled his bull-like shoulders. "If there's trouble around here, I'm the hombre what'll bring it about." He narrowed his eyes. "You and George get your lazy carcasses over to Santa Fe. You can get there by dark. Find Bratcher. He hangs out at that cantina beside the livery on the north side of the square. I want a dozen hardcases here in the morning. Fifty dollars a week until the job's done."

Dowd nodded, then glanced furtively at Scruggs. He cleared his throat. "What if he ain't there, Zeke?"

Faber's eyes narrowed with an unspoken threat. "Then don't come back." He glared at them, then cut his eyes to Dink. "Come with me."

When Faber and Dink entered the mayor's office, John Rawlings looked up from behind the cherry wood desk he had freighted in from New Hampshire. He rose from his chair and smiled expansively. "Sheriff Faber. What a surprise. Always good to see you." He nodded politely to Dink.

Faber growled, "Drop the act, Rawlings. Dink here is one of my boys from the Cooper spread. He's got a story to tell and you best listen. Go ahead, Dink."

A frown knit the businessman's forehead. He glanced at Dink, then back to the sheriff. He slowly sat in his chair and nodded. "I'm listening."

Rawlings' face remained impassive as Dink related the events of the last few days. "Zeke said that you and the sheriff should get up an army because that bearded jasper is Cleve Bollinger, the gunfighter."

Lifting an eyebrow slightly, Rawlings looked up at the sheriff, puzzled. "So, what's the problem?"

Sheriff Faber leaned forward, his big hands spread on the desk. "The problem is that if this is Bollinger, it's bad news. You ain't from around here, Rawlings, but ten years or so back, from what I've heard, no man in this part of the territory could match Bollinger with fists or guns."

Shifting his cool gaze between Faber and the young gunman, Rawlings replied. "Last I heard, we have almost twenty hired guns out at the ranch. No man is a match for twenty gunhands."

Dink spoke up. "Not twenty no more, Mister Rawlings. There be eleven now, counting me."

Rawlings's frown deepened. "Eleven? What happened?"

"Bollinger," Faber growled. "He's done got rid of almost half the crew. We got to run him down. Him and that old man, Cooper. We been putting off, figuring the old man would give up and pack his worthless hide out of the territory, but we ain't got the time now to wait. Hombres like Bollinger can come in and rip out your guts before you even see him."

"That's hard to believe, Sheriff," said Rawlings skeptically. He held up his hand to halt Faber's retort. "But, I won't argue with you. Do what you think you must."

A smug grin twisted Faber's rugged square face. "Good. Best you get ready to open that safe of yours. I got a dozen gunnies riding in tomorrow. I already sent for them."

With a nod, the businessman muttered, "Are they good?"

"The best money can buy. Fifty a week until they take care of Cooper and Bollinger."

Rawlings opened the oak wood humidor and retrieved

a black cigar. "That's quite a large sum of money," he muttered as he opened the desk drawer and pulled out a silver cigar clipper.

Sheriff Faber snorted. "Call it an investment on the biggest payday you and me have ever seen."

"As long as they got the stomach to make sure the job is done right."

Faber chuckled. "Don't worry, Rawlings. These old boys would shoot their own mother for a gold eagle."

Chapter Twenty-one

Shifting the wad of tobacco to the other cheek, Sam Cooper leaned back against the granite wall of the cave and stared into the fire as Jorge Castel completed the message he brought.

The old man's ears burned with rage and frustration. He cursed his own weakness. Maybe someday he would learn to rein in his temper, but that blasted son of his could always rile him up something fierce. If he had stayed calm, maybe he could have talked the hot-headed boy out of his impossible pursuit.

Rising from where she was sitting behind the men as was the custom of the Owinos, Maria took a step forward. "*Por favor, mi padre*, go to your son. He must have our help if he is to do as he set out."

Cooper looked up at his daughter, the firelight flickering on the smooth bronze skin of her cheeks. She looked

167

so much like her mother. Wearily, he shook his head. "We ain't a match for the sheriff. That's what I tried to tell Clint. If I send our people against them, all I will accomplish is sending them to their graves."

Her black eyes flashed with anger. "At least, they would die fighting for that which belongs to them." She glared at her father for several moments, her black eyes flashing defiance before dropping her gaze to the hard floor of the cave.

Cooper cut his eyes sharply at her, and then his brows knit as a sense of remorse flooded over him. He had to admit that his bluff had failed. He had hoped by refusing to help Clint, the mule-headed cuss would think twice about tackling Rawlings and Faber. But he hadn't.

The old man grimaced. He should have remembered the arguments he and Clint had over the years, arguments that neither father nor son won, arguments that sometimes brought about days of silence between the two stubborn men.

Rising to his feet, he fumbled in his pocket for a twist of tobacco. He tore off a chunk and announced. "I'll not send a single *vaquero,* but I will go, and I will take those who wish to ride with me."

The frown vanished from Maria's face. With a squeal of delight, she threw her arms around his neck.

"Hold on there, *poco uno*. You're going to choke me certain, and then I sure ain't going to be able to pull Clint's bacon out of the fire," he grumbled brusquely.

She dropped her arms to her side and smiled up at him. He touched a gnarled finger to her cheek, then limped over to the bear hide and pulled it open. "Luiz. I'm riding to the *hacienda* come morning. Any *vaquero* who wants to ride with me best be here, or he'll get left behind. And tell them to come heeled with enough artillery to sway their backs."

Next morning squatting by the small fire in the mouth of his cave and sipping a cup of six-shooter coffee, Clint studied the *hacienda.* There was no sign of activity. Just after noon, two riders emerged from the foothills south of the compound, pushing a dozen or so ponies ahead of them.

An hour later, the stable door swung open and ten riders emerged, half heading for the south road out of the valley, half for the north.

Speck grunted. "What do you reckon they got on their minds now?"

Clint frowned. "No telling." He sipped his coffee. "Let's just wait until they play a card."

Zeke played his first card twenty minutes later when the first band of gunman hit the north road. The hardcases spread out and turned west through the pine and fir forests.

"Looks like they plan on searching the foothills again," Speck drawled a few minutes later as the group of riders to the south also turned west.

Clint chuckled. "They never learn." He sighed deeply and pushed himself to his feet. "I reckon it's time for us to get to work. Let's shut things down here." He pointed to a granite outcropping at the timberline several hundred feet above. "We'll move our gear up there. I ran across a cave behind a twisted pine. Got a live spring inside. It comes out on the other side of the ridge. We can see anyone that comes within a half-mile, and need be, can dart out the back with no one the wiser."

From the outcropping, Clint pointed out the riders to the south as they rode through a meadow surrounded by golden aspen. He grinned at Speck. "Let's go down and make them welcome."

Thirty minutes later, Clint reined up behind a row of jagged granite on the crest of a ridge. "There they are," he whispered, nodding to the five riders descending the slope on the far ridge about a half-mile distant, heading directly toward them. "You got that Spencer unlimbered?"

Speck patted the stock of the .52 rifle in the boot. "She'll be ready."

Clint shucked his '66 Winchester, a rimfire with twenty-eight grains of powder pushing the .44 caliber slug, and dismounted. He tied his gray tightly. "Find a spot, and let's howdy them."

After they situated themselves behind the saw-toothed rocks on the slope, Clint nodded to a clearing about fifty yards below. "When they get to the middle of that clearing, knock up a chunk of dirt in front of them with that big boomer of yours." He grinned at Speck. "Think you can manage to do that?"

The freckle-faced cowboy shrugged and grinned. "Maybe."

The riders paused at the base of the slope, giving their ponies a short rest and a drink from the icy stream rushing down the mountainside.

Up above, Speck rolled over on his side and grinned wryly at Clint. "I sure could use a cigarette."

Clint grinned at the devious comment. "I'll roll one too."

Speck chuckled. "You're pretty sneaky, you know?"

Clint's grin broadened. "Look who's talking. You're the jasper what brought it up."

"You know they'll smell the smoke."

"So they smell it. Where they going to run that we can't get to them with these saddleguns?" He rolled over on his back and pulled out his bag of Bull Durham. Moments later, he stuck the cigarette between his lips and pulled out a match. He glanced at Speck. "Ready?"

Speck held up a match. "Ready."

Together, they touched the flames to their cigarettes and inhaled deeply, then blew the smoke into the air. The air rising up the slope caught the smoke, swirled it upward where the down currents swept it to the bottom of the slope.

Speck chuckled and blew another puff of smoke.

Clint rolled back onto his stomach and peered down the slope. The riders were almost to the clearing. One reined up, holding his hand over his head. They were still too distant to hear the words, but the way the riders sniffed the air made it clear enough they smelled the cigarette smoke.

For several seconds, an animated discussion took place among the five until finally, they continued their ascent of the slope.

"Ain't one of them jaspers a deputy?" Speck asked.

"Looks like."

Speck removed the cigarette from his lips, laid it on the rocks beside him, and lined up the nickel-steel front blade on a Stetson-sized boulder in the middle of the clearing. "Tell me when," he muttered.

Down below, the riders were still sniffing the air.

"Now," Clint whispered.

The Spencer roared, its thunder echoing off the ridges surrounding the valley. The boulder disintegrated into thousands of sharp granite shards, sending the startled horses exploding into frantic spasms of sun-fishing and cloud-hunting while the cursing riders clung to their ponies with all their might. Finally they managed to calm their horses.

Clint called down the slope. "Next one means business."

Willy glanced around. "Hold on, Mister. We're not looking for trouble. We was just out hunting."

Clint rose to his feet, holding his Winchester at his waist with the muzzle on the riders. "Hunting what?"

"Bear, deer—just looking for some meat."

Hatchet-faced Nolan Martin began to ease his pony aside.

Clint stopped him "Stay where you are, partner. I'm

not playing games. I sure ain't anxious to kill nobody, but I dearly promise you a piece of ground if you don't ride out of this valley. And I mean now."

Deputy John Drucker sneered. "You talk mighty brave seeing we got you five to one."

"Make that two," Speck drawled, pushing to his feet.

Martin's eyes narrowed on Clint. "You be Bollinger."

"Could be."

Martin sneered. "You don't look so tough."

"Maybe not, but tough enough to handle sheep dip like you waddies." Clint shifted the muzzle of his Winchester to the left slightly, centered right in the middle of Martin's chest.

For several seconds, the two sides glared at each other. A sense of frustration welled in Clint, for he knew the longer they faced each other, the more likely the hardcases were to spin the wheel. In a soft voice, Clint said, "No sense in you dying just for a few dollars. Turn them ponies around and ride out the valley. That's all you got to do."

"I'll see you in hades first," shouted Willy, grabbing for his six-gun.

The slope exploded with gunfire.

Clint's slug sent Martin tumbling over the rump of his horse. From the corner of his eye, he saw Willy throw up his arms and his body twist as the powerful 350-grain slug from the Spencer tore his body from the saddle.

He dropped to his knees and jerked the muzzle around at the other three who had thrown up their hands and were shaking their heads, pleading with Clint and Speck not to shoot.

The blood fury from the old days pounded in Clint's skull, but he held his finger lightly on the trigger. From somewhere beyond the hammering of the blood, he heard the frantic screams. "Don't shoot, Bollinger. Don't shoot. We'll leave. It ain't worth getting kilt over," shouted Drucker.

"Then git. And take those vermin with you."

Moments later as the three men spurred their ponies down the slope leading the horses with the dead bodies, Speck glanced at Clint. "You all right?"

Clint looked around, noting the concern on his partner's slender face. He forced a grin. "Yeah. Now, let's get back up to our camp and make sure those jaspers light a shuck out of this valley."

On the north side of the valley, Zeke led his four men, including the Bodines, through the forest, up and down hogback ridges, fording swiftly moving streams, and clattering across rock slides.

Zeke reined up when he heard distant gunshots. As suddenly as they had erupted, they grew silent, and within moments their echoes had died away.

"What do you think, Zeke?"

Zeke glanced at his hired gun and shrugged. "Not much telling."

"Think Drucker and them got Bollinger?" The hard-case grunted. "Just my luck. I could have sure used that two hundred—" a gagging sound cut off his words.

Zeke heard a sharp thud and jerked around to see the gunhand clutching at his blood–soaked neck. Then Zeke saw the arrow between the man's fingers, an arrow with a sharpened point and three white feathers.

Chapter Twenty-two

Muttering an oath, Zeke grabbed his six-gun and wheeled his pony about, his black eyes frantically searching the silent forest around him. He thought he glimpsed a shadow fleeting among the thick trunks of lodgepole pine and disappearing into a stand of new growth fir. He snapped off a shot. "Over there," he shouted, firing again.

Instantly, a deafening barrage of gunfire erupted.

Seconds later, Al screamed and grabbed at an arrow protruding from the fleshy part of his shoulder. "Apaches," he hollered, yanking out the arrow and spurring his horse around.

"I'm getting out of here," Pete shouted.

Zeke jerked his head around. "No! Get back here, blast you." But it was too late. The three Bodines were setting a blistering trail back to the *hacienda*. He heard a groan and a soft thud behind him. He jerked around frantically only to see that the wounded gunman had fallen from the saddle.

Blood gurgling in his throat, the frightened cowboy looked up at Zeke. His words came in gasps. "Zeke–help–me–please–help."

Zeke heard no more for he wheeled his horse about and dug wicked spurs into the animal's flanks, sending him bolting after the Bodines who were already a quarter of a mile away. "Ain't no way I'm staying out here with a bunch of wild Apaches," he muttered between clenched teeth.

Pausing on a ridge overlooking the valley, Speck frowned at the distant gunfire. "What do you reckon is going on over there? Them jaspers stumble on each other?" He chuckled.

Clint grinned. "Likely as not, Ojo stumbled on them."

The three waddies Clint had sent packing stopped at the hacienda long enough to drop off the horses with their gruesome loads, then skedaddled for the north road back to El Jardin. Halfway across the valley, they met the Bodines who joined them in their flight.

When Zeke emerged from the forest, he spotted the six riders hightailing it out of the valley. He reined up and looked over his shoulder, then glanced at the *hacienda.* He shook his head. "This ain't for me. Faber can have it. Ain't no way I'm hanging around here all by my lonesome," he growled, digging the spurs into his pony and racing after his men.

Speck clapped Clint on the shoulder. "Well, partner. Looks like we lit a fire in them jaspers' britches."

Clint chuckled. "Sure looks that way." He studied the riders disappearing up the north road. "Reckon we might as well pick up our plunder and sleep under a roof tonight. Leave the dynamite. Might still need it."

"A roof sounds good to me." Speck clicked his tongue, sending his yellow dun scrambling down the slope. He drew up. "Hold on. What if them jaspers decide to come back. Two of us can't hold them off."

Pursing his lips, Clint nodded. "I thought about that. I don't figure they will, but just in case, we'll stable our horses in the cave leading to the tunnel. Trouble comes up, we slip out and no one's the wiser."

Sam Cooper rode out with twenty *vaqueros* behind him, armed with an odd assortment of ancient Army Colts, shotguns, percussion muskets, bell-mouthed *escopetas*, and even two or three Spanish pikes. Cooper, his *cargador*, Luiz, and three *vaqueros* packed Yellow Boy Henrys.

Following the same hidden trail Maria had journeyed leading Clint and Speck to the *rancho,* the large band made slow time. Mid-day, a young vaquero raced up and pointed to the west. "*Usted mira, el Patron*. Look. *Muchos vaqueros* on the road."

For several moments, the old man stared at the pine and fir covered slopes in the distance. He nodded to

Luiz. "Send Juan and Antonio to see who rides there. We wait here. Let whoever it be get ahead of us. Tell the *vaqueros* no fires to give away our presence."

After rounding the first bend in the north road where he was out of sight of the valley, Pete spotted the sentry cabin ahead. He reined up. The other riders pulled up.

The two sentries emerged from the cabin just as Zeke caught up with them. "What's going on?" He asked. "What are you stopping for?"

Pete nodded to the cabin. "We're staying here." Al and Joe looked at each other. Joe shrugged

"What's up?" Asked one of the sentries.

"Bollinger!" exclaimed Zeke.

Deputy Drucker stared at Zeke, then Bodine. He nodded to his two compadres. "Not me. I ain't staying here. We just dropped Willy and Nolan off at the *hacienda*, both of them deader than a beaver hat. I ain't joining them." He backed his pony away, then spurred him down the road, followed by the other two owlhoots.

Zeke hesitated, staring at Pete. Finally, he shook his head. "I ain't staying. You old boys is crazy if you do." He glanced down at the two puzzled sentries. "And you're crazy if you stay."

For several moments, the two sentries stared at each other, then hastily saddled their ponies and raced after Zeke.

The Bodines watched as the two disappeared down the road. Joe turned to his brother. "I didn't want to say nothing in front of them, Pete, but there ain't no reason for us to hang around here. We got some of the sheriff's money. Forget the rest. Let's ride."

Pete ignored the question. He pulled up beside Al and looked at the blood-soaked hole in the shoulder of the heavy Mackinaw. "You hurt?"

"Naw. Punched a hole, but didn't bust nothing. Coat was too heavy. So, now what? We staying here or going back?"

A sneer curled Pete's broad lips. "I want the rest of that five hundred dollars." He glanced up into a sky painted blood red by the setting sun. "We'll stay the night here and ride back in the morning."

Joe drew a deep breath. "I still say we just keep on riding. What with the cash we had on us, we probably got close to a thousand dollars now."

The sneer on Pete's rugged face grew wider. "You ride on if you've got such a mind, little brother. I swore I'd get this jasper, and that's just what I'm going to do."

Shaking his head, Joe sighed. "No. I'll stay."

"All right. Take the horses in the corral. I'll tend to our brother."

Staying within the forest, Clint and Speck rode around the perimeter of the valley toward the *hacienda* when they spotted Ojo Blanco and Strong Swimmer.

"You have been busy," Clint remarked. "We heard gunfire."

Ojo Blanco frowned. "Only one die." He grunted. "Maybe like my woman say, Ojo Blanco is getting old."

"No. Ojo Blanco is great warrior. I am grateful for his help."

The old warrior nodded, and Clint even spotted a flicker of a smile on Strong Swimmer's lips. "We ride to *hacienda*. You are welcome."

He grew solemn. "No. We follow those who flee. One of them is the one who killed Hair Rope."

Clint felt a cold hand seize his head. "Hair Rope. I thought he went back for help."

Ojo Blanco shook his head briefly. "That same night, the one named Drucker shot Hair Rope from ambush. We kill him tonight."

Remembering the distant shot he had heard the night before, Clint held up his hand in a sign of peace. "I understand."

Clint and Speck rode into the *hacienda*. Reining up at the hitching rail in front of the stone house, Clint remained in the saddle staring down at several curious Mexican laborers and servants. "*Hable ingles?*"

Several of the Mexicans exchanged guilty looks with each other until one stepped forward and shook his head. "*No ingles.*"

With a wry grin at their poor attempt at deception, he pointed to his chest. "*El hijo de tonelero de* Sam Cooper."

Hearing the grizzled cowpoke claim he was the son of Sam Cooper, *Señora* Inez pushed through the cluster of curious servants with her daughter. She peered up into Clint's face. With a trace of fear in her eyes, she studied him. "*Señor* Cleve?"

Clint studied her a moment, trying to place the familiar features of her face. He nodded. "*Si*. Cleve. Son of

Sam Cooper." Then he remembered her. "Inez? *Señora* Inez, the gentle one," he said.

Her eyes lit with joy. He was the son of Sam, for young Cleve was the only one ever to call her such. "*Señor* Cleve! We thought you . . ." She paused, making the sign of the cross.

He laughed. "Not quite, *Señora*. And who is this young one at your side? This couldn't be Damita, the little baby princess." He leaned over and held his hand out to the side of the stirrup. "She was only this tall when I last saw her."

"*Si, Señor* Cleve, *Si*. This is Damita," she exclaimed proudly, pushing the blushing young girl forward. The smile on her face faded momentarily when she looked past him. "*El Patron*. He is with you?"

Clint dismounted. "No. But he will come soon."

Her face flattened with fear. "You must leave. Many *malo* hombres are here. They are evil, cursed by *el Diablo*."

He gestured to Speck. "We have met them, *Señora*. They run like cowards up the north road. We stay here."

She nodded briskly, then spoke to those around her rapidly. Smiles leaped to their faces. They surged forward, laughing and chattering.

"Come," Inez said. "Eat. We take your horses to the stable. Do not concern yourself."

Clint hesitated. "But first, I must ask your help."

Her face grew hard. She searched the crowd around them, spotting the sly face of Chochiti. She shook her head. "Not here. Come. The salon."

While they put themselves around a hot meal of sliced peppered beef rolled in tortillas and doused with a hot salsa not even *el Diablo* could handle, *Señora* Inez explained. "The one they call Chochiti, he is one of *Señor* Turner's dogs. All he hears or sees, he gives to them."

Speck arched an eyebrow. "Seems mighty unhealthy to have a jasper like that around. Were it me, I'd be inclined to remedy the situation."

A conspiratorial gleam flickered in *Señora* Inez's black eyes. "Trust me, *Señor*. With the *malo* hombres gone, Chochiti has no friends. He will regret what he has done." She paused, her dark complexioned features wrinkled in concern. "But, what of the law, *Señor* Cleve? Does it seek you?" Her gaze involuntarily flicked to the hoglegs on his hips.

Clint chuckled. "The law believes I am dead. That is why I go by another name, *Señora*."

"Ah." Her brows suddenly knit with a frown. "There is something you must know, *Señor* Cleve. The one, Turner, he believes you are the son of *el Patron*." Her black eyes flashed. "He threaten to kill my *nina* if I do not answer his questions."

Frowning, Clint studied her. "He only believes I live. He does not know for certain."

She nodded vigorously. "*Si*."

With a grin, he said, "Then do not worry over it, *si?*"

She smiled. "*Si*. Now, what is it I can do for you?"

"Send a message to my father. Tell him we have the *hacienda* and for him to come a running."

"I will send Vincentes."

"Good. One more thing. Can you find someone you trust to stable our horses in the escape tunnel."

She frowned. "The tunnel, but . . ."

Clint explained. "Maria showed us the tunnel. If this Turner comes back, we don't want to be trapped inside."

She nodded. "I hide them. I go tonight. And do not worry, I will be unseen."

At that moment, a peon in a baggy shirt and pants rushed in. "*Señora!*. Chochiti is gone. He take a horse and leave."

A worried frown wrinkled her face.

"What is wrong?" Clint asked.

"Chochiti. He hear that you are the son of Sam Cooper."

Speck cursed. "There goes our secret."

Chapter Twenty-three

Chochiti rode hard. He reined up when he hit the north road, scenting the pungent odor of wood smoke. He eased into the forest and went on foot, wary of who might be ahead.

Minutes later, he spotted the cabin. Falling to his hands and knees, he crept closer until he could peer through the gunport in the shuttered window. To his surprise, it was the three brothers, the Bodines, sitting in from of a small fire in the adobe fireplace.

The younger brother was arguing. "I still say we should take what money Faber gave us and ride out of the country. Head up to the northern territories."

"Is that what you think, Al?" Pete glared at his brother who was tending his shoulder.

"Me, I don't care one way or another. Wherever we

end up, we're going to find trouble. Might as well be here as Montany."

The cunning Mexican listened as the brothers argued, and as he stood crouched there in the cold, an idea came to him. Silently, he slipped back through the forest to his pony.

A few minutes later, the Bodine brothers heard hoofbeats. Guns drawn, they peered thorough the gunports. It was Chochiti. He feigned surprise when they stepped from the cabin. He quickly explained what had taken place back at the *hacienda*. With Turner's men gone, he figured his health would be better if he left.

Pete snorted. "Well, at least you're one greaser who ain't so dumb."

Chochiti grinned slyly. "This man, Bowles, *Señor.* You do not much like him, *si*?"

Al leaned back against the cabin and pulled out a bag of Bull Durham. "Reckon you got that right, Mex. Pete hates his guts."

"Yep," Pete growled, patting the hogleg on his hip. "If I could get that jasper in my sights, I'd make short work of him."

"That ain't likely anytime soon," Al grunted. "He's boarded up behind them stone walls, and he ain't coming out just to say howdy."

His devious mind clicking, the diminutive Mexican said. "If there was a way into the *hacienda,* would the *señor* find it in his heart to perhaps offer a few pesos?"

Pete frowned, then grinned, elated. "I knew it. There had to be a way in. Do you know where it is?"

Chochiti shrugged. "Perhaps." He paused. Looked up from under his eyebrows, he added, "For a price."

Al's face went black with rage. "For a price? Why you sneaky little—"

"Hold on, Al." Pete broke in. "Hold on. Let's hear what the greaser has to say."

In a whining voice, Chochiti said. "It is not for me, *patron*, but *mi madre* in El Jardin. She is—*enfermo*—how do you say it, ill. I ask for little, just enough for *el doctor*."

Al sputtered. "Let's beat it out of him, Pete. I'll find out what he knows."

Chochiti backed his pony away.

Uncharacteristically patient, Pete held up hand. "Hold it, Al. The Mex has information we need. After all," he continued, winking at his brother. "You can't blame a man for wanting to make a dollar, now can you? Besides, like the good son he is, he's only wanting to help out his ma."

Al frowned, then grinned as the devious intent of his brother became evident. "No. I reckon you can't."

Pete turned to the diminutive man. "How much and when do we see it."

Chochiti lowered his head, doing his best to appear meek and reluctant. "*Mi madre,* she is very ill. Perhaps, if the *señor* is most gracious—fifty American dollars."

"I reckon we can handle that." Pete pulled out his cash and peeled off fifty dollars. "Now, when do we see it?"

Stunned by the immense fortune dropped in his hands, Chochiti exclaimed. "We go now. Enough snow remains that we may see until the moon rises."

While the Bodines saddled their ponies, Chochiti built three torches to light their way through the tunnel.

Earlier, when the sun began to drop and the mountain air took on a sharp edge, Sheriff Faber shivered inside his heavy fur-lined coat, despite the exertion of the forced ride. He glanced over his shoulder at the blood red sky and cursed. He had planned to reach the ranch before dark, but Dowd and Scruggs didn't arrive in El Jardin with Frank Bratcher and his nine hired killers until well after noon.

Dowd rode up beside the sheriff. "Getting late, Sheriff."

Faber ignored his suggestion.

They rode on in silence for another mile.

Suddenly, Faber reined up, throwing up his arm to halt the riders behind him. He peered into the darkness of the road before him and cocked his head to listen. Far in the distance came the pounding of hoof beats. He shucked his six-gun just as Zeke rounded a bend with several riders following.

When Zeke spotted the small army, he jerked his horse to a halt.

Faber's face darkened when he recognized Zeke. "Where in the blazes do you think you're going?" He kept the muzzle of his hogleg on Zeke's belly.

The other riders pulled up beside Zeke. Drucker

said, "Anywhere but back in the valley. I got my belly full of trouble back there."

Faber's eyes grew cold. "Well, Drucker," he drawled, shifting the muzzle of his six-gun to the cowboy's belly. "You got a heap of trouble right here. What you got to decide is if you want to face it here or back there."

Drucker sat stiffly in the saddle, his eyes boring into Faber's, testing the resolve of the sheriff. He saw no sign of indecision, only a hard, cold determination.

With a sheepish grin, he sat back in his saddle. "I reckon I'd sooner tangle with the trouble back there, Sheriff."

Faber nodded sharply. The red sky began to gray. Cold shadows fell over the road. "We'll spend the night here," he barked. "Ride out at first light. What happened back there?"

From where he lay on the needles behind tall pines high on the slope above the narrow road, Juan Rodriguez studied the scattered fires below, searching the darkness between the fires hoping to see some sign of Antonio Cortez who had slipped down the slope to learn the identity and purpose of the band of hard-looking gun hands.

Upon Cooper's orders, the two *vaqueros* had been following the riders for the last two hours, waiting for an opportunity to learn more.

Juan was growing anxious. Antonio had been gone over an hour.

Suddenly, a soft rustle sounded from below and with it a soft hiss. "Juan. It is I."

"*Apuro*! Hurry! *El Patron*, he waits for us."

At the same time, Chochiti led the Bodines along the edge of the forest to the river, then through the trees lining the riverbank up to within half a mile of the tunnel. "We go on foot. The *caballos* will reveal our presence."

Cutting up the arroyo, they finally reached the mouth of the tunnel where the slightly built Mexican lighted the torches and led the way inside.

To his surprise, two horses, a yellow dun and a gray, were stabled in the tunnel. Pete snorted. "Looks like our boys was looking for a sneaky way out." A mocking leer twisted his lips and a cruel gleam filled his eyes. "Well, they ain't going to be needing these broomtails no more," he growled, whipping out his skinning knife. In two swift strokes, he slashed the animals' throats.

Pete and Al laughed at the animals squealing and thrashing about on the floor of the cave. Joe turned his head away, trying to still the gorge rising in his throat. Chochiti's eyes grew wide and his face paled, suddenly terrified of the cruel gringos.

At the stairs leading up to the storeroom, Chochiti paused. "The stairs lead to the storeroom and then to the *cocino*, the kitchen as you call it. Soon the sun will rise. I must go."

He turned to leave, but Pete hooked his arm around the smaller man's neck and plunged the eight-inch skinning knife in his back, severing his spine and killing him instantly.

He knelt by the dead man's side, dug through his pockets for the fifty dollars, then led the way upstairs. "Come on, brothers. We got us two snakes to kill."

In the kitchen, they paused. Back to the east, the first graying of false dawn lit the sky. "Won't be long now," Pete growled. "Don't make no noise. I figure on finding Bowle's room. I want that jasper to be awake so he'll know who's killing him."

In Sam Cooper's camp high in the mountains, Juan and Antonio squatted by the fire gnawing on broiled rabbit and relating what they had seen.

The morning air was crisp and sharp enough to send a chill into the bones. "Sheriff Faber, huh?" Sam drawled, loosing an arc of tobacco and peering into the dark forest in the direction of the sheriff.

"*Si, el Patron*," replied Antonio. "I count *catorce*, maybe *quince* gringos. With much mean looks in their faces and many guns in their hands. One of the *hombres malos* was a gringo called Turner."

Cooper leaned forward. "Zeke Turner?" The young Mexican *vaquero* nodded. He shook his head. "I'll be hornswoggled. That could only mean one thing. The boys done run him out of the valley." He grunted and stared at the fire. "I would never have believed it." He fixed Antonio with a hard look. "You're certain, dead certain it was Turner."

"*Si, el Patron*. I remember Turner. He is the one who

gave me this," he replied, rolling up his sleeve to reveal the scar of a bullet wound.

Cooper nodded. "You did well, Antonio, Juan. *Gracias*." He rose stiffly to his feet and wandered into the night, followed by his shadow, Luiz. He stared into the darkness.

Knowing that Clint and his partner were probably at the *hacienda* and ripe for surprise by the sheriff's band of fourteen or fifteen killers made the old man rethink his plans. He felt the presence of Luiz at his side. Without looking at his ramrod, he said. "We're no match for the sheriff, my friend, but somehow, we got to find us a way to even the odds."

"*Si, Patron*. What shall we do?"

Cooper shook his head. And then the idea struck him. "We're breaking camp, Luiz. Tell the *vaqueros*."

Chapter Twenty-four

Half-a-dozen fires in a circle marked Faber's camp. Drucker rolled out his bedroll near one. As his habit, he slept with his six-gun in his hand. From time to time, someone would toss on another few branches to replenish the fire, but in the early morning hours when sleep is the soundest, the fires burned low.

In the middle of a lascivious dream, sudden pressure on his mouth jerked him awake. He looked up into the snarling face of Strong Swimmer as the Apache warrior plunged a knife into his heart and twisted it, all the while holding a callused hand over the owlhoot's mouth so he couldn't scream. His legs jerked, kicking once or twice. His body went rigid in fear, contracting the muscles in his finger, which squeezed the trigger.

Strong Swimmer slumped across Drucker, but the deputy could not feel the weight for he was already dead.

In the darkness beyond the fire, Ojo Blanco watched impassively. The struggle awakened the camp, and as the first cowboy ran to investigate the commotion, the old warrior drove a yard-long arrow through his neck, and the next two cowpokes that jerked to a halt by the bodies, then disappeared into the Sangre de Cristos without a trace.

Hair Rope had been avenged, but at a terrible price.

Speck's eyes popped open. He stared into the darkness of the ceiling, wondering what had awakened him. He listened intently.

Nothing.

He turned on his side, but sleep evaded him. Muttering a curse, he rolled out of bed and slipped on his trousers. He reached for his boots, shaking his head when he realized he had neglected to arrange them according to his nightly routine, heels together, toes facing east. He grimaced. Bad luck.

He chuckled to himself. Maybe Clint was right. Maybe superstitions were nonsense, but Speck reminded himself, he had been following them for years, and he was getting too old to change now.

Stomping into his boots, he strapped on his gun-belt.

Clint growled from the other bunk. "Can't you make some more noise? I'm trying to sleep."

Speck chuckled and reached for the door. "Go on back to sleep. I'm putting the coffee on." He stepped into the hall and froze.

Less than thirty feet away in the middle of the salon, stood the Bodine brothers, lit by the dim flickering of the oil lamps on the walls.

Speck's sudden appearance startled the Bodines, giving the freckle-faced cowpoke just enough time to draw and fire as he threw himself to the floor of the hall and rolled under a bench. "Clint! It's Bodine!"

In the next instant, the salon and hallway exploded in gunfire.

Clint leaped from his bunk, grabbing both his .36s' and threw open the door. Smoke was growing thick in the hallway. He glanced over his shoulder.

The window.

Quickly, he threw open the shutter and dived out headfirst into the snow. Once outside, he raced to the glass doors opening into the salon. Without hesitation, he lowered his shoulder and crashed through the glass, landing on his back and rolling over, six-guns belching yellow plumes of flame.

Startled by the shattering doors, Al jerked around, a savage snarl on his face. Clint put two slugs into his heart, spinning him around and onto the flagstone-tiled floor.

Crouched behind the heavy table, Pete cursed and leaped to his feet, his square face dark with rage. Clint rolled to his right as the big man fired, tearing up chunks of white flagstone.

Clint rolled to his stomach and fired twice, both slugs catching Bodine in the chest. In the next moment, Clint rolled back to his left and fired twice more.

Bodine's head snapped back. His dying reflexes squeezing the trigger of his six-gun as he slammed to the floor.

The slug whistled just above Clint's head. A startled cry from behind Clint jerked him around. Joe was leaning against the wall, both hands holding his bloody belly and staring in disbelief at the body of his brother. "P—Pete," he gasped, slowly sliding down the wall to a sitting position on the floor. "You killed me, Pete. You killed me."

Back at Cooper's camp on the mountain, Juan rode out to warn Clint and Speck of the sheriff's approach. "Don't get on the road until you be well past that bunch down there," Sam cautioned the young man. "Tell Clint about the escape tunnel. You know the cave in the foothills west of the valley?" Juan nodded. "That's where we'll meet you. *Comprende?*"

"*Si, el Patron.* Do not concern yourself. I will give them your word."

A worried grin split the old man's face. "Take care." He glanced around at Luiz. "Now, let's slow the sheriff down."

Departing from the regular trail over the mountains, Cooper took the shorter route, a narrow and treacherous trail along the face of the basaltic rock slopes that led them to Devil's Bluff, a sheer precipice looking down on the road where it was pinched between the bluff and a canyon wall.

Luiz expressed his concern for the danger of the

route, but Cooper continued pushing hard. "If we reach the bluff before Faber's men, we can even out the odds," he replied. "We'll have them trapped."

The eyes of the swarthy *vaquero* lit up. He grinned.

Juan never reached the road.

He reined up on the crest of a ridge overlooking the winding road, guessing he was a mile, maybe two from the sheriff's camp. To the east, the sky was beginning to gray. He urged his wiry pony down the steep slope. Without warning, a dead branch snapped from a lodge-pole pine and plummeted to the ground, landing right in front of the little mustang.

Startled, the animal reared, squealing and pawing the air.

Rodriguez fought for control, but the frightened pony spun and reared again, this time falling over backwards. Exclaiming a prayerful oath, the *vaquero* leaped from the saddle, but his big-roweled spur caught in the cinch. The thrashing mustang fell on him, shattering his leg. He screamed in agony as the pony struggled to its feet and bolted through the pine and fir, dragging the hapless Mexican after him.

Juan's head slammed into the thick trunk of a pine. The impact tore his spur from the cinch, and he rolled limply against a small boulder as his pony vanished into the forest.

"We're in time," Cooper muttered, staring over the rim of the precipice. The first vestiges of false dawn were beginning to lighten the eastern sky above the mountain peaks.

He placed the *vaqueros* along the rim with instructions not to fire until he gave the command. He returned to his position and waited, well aware that the inferior weapons and poor marksmanship of his *vaqueros* offered little chance of a successful ambush, but at least it would send a message to Faber that he and his hired guns were not alone in the mountains.

Back in the *hacienda,* Clint checked the three Bodines just to make sure they were not playing possum.

"Dead?" Speck's voice cracked as he shuffled through the smoke clutching his left arm.

Clint holstered his .36s and hurried to his partner. "Is it bad?"

Speck shook his head. "Naw. Didn't hit no bone. Reckon it'll be a little stiff, but that's all."

Señora Inez hurried in, her eyes wide in shock at the men sprawled on the floor. She looked at Clint in concern.

He laughed. "We're fine, *Señora.* Speck here needs his arm bandaged. Find some hands to haul these jaspers out and bury them."

She nodded and turned to the *sirvientes* behind her. She rattled off a rapid set of orders, and the menservants rushed to carry out her instructions. She called out to her husband. "Diego!" She gestured to the double doors. "Board the door." He nodded and trotted away, and then she waved at the women. "*Vamanos.* Make the fire. These men are hungry."

Speck shook his head. "Not me. Just coffee."

Clint nodded. "Same here."

While the *señora* skillfully tended Speck's arm, he shook his head. "I should have figured some trouble when I put on my boots this morning," he announced.

Clint rolled his eyes. "Don't tell me. You didn't have the toes pointing east."

Speck raised an eyebrow, then glanced at his wound. "Don't fun me on this. They wasn't pointing east, and it brought me back luck. You can't argue that."

Before Clint could reply, Damita, the little baby princess, brought their coffee.

"You best start believing in some of them superstitions, Clint," said Speck after taking a sip of coffee. "You might keep us out of some trouble."

After ordering his deputy's body tossed in an arroyo, Sheriff Faber broke camp and continued the journey to the valley. A few minutes later, Dowd pointed out a riderless mustang grazing along the side of the narrow road. The deputy rode over and picked the animal up.

Faber studied the saddle and rigging. The silver conchas that decorated the saddle fenders and the bridle revealed the culture of the owner.

"Mex," muttered Dowd.

Faber searched the mountain slopes on either side, seeing nothing, a disturbing experience for always on the journey to the valley, he would meet a few Mexican peons trudging beside their burros or *carretas*, but so far on this journey, this pony was the first evidence of their presence. That worried him.

Dowd grunted. "Handsome saddle."

He glanced tentatively at Faber who shrugged. "Take it."

With a grin, Dowd tied the reins to his pommel, and they continued toward the valley.

A few miles farther, Faber reined up when he spotted Devil's Bluff. The quarter-mile stretch of road pinched between the bluff and the canyon wall portended certain death in the event or a landslide or an ambush. Although he had never experienced either incident, the sheriff always kicked his pony into a brisk canter to cover the stretch as quickly as possible.

Bratcher rode up beside him. "What's wrong now?"

Rolling his broad shoulders, the sheriff continued studying the bluff. "I ain't sure, but I got a feeling. What with that Mexican pony wandering around with no owner—" He looked at Bratcher. "Well, sir, I figure we might just ought to unleather our handguns and be ready for anything."

Bratcher's thick eyebrows lifted in surprise. He snorted, then sneered. "You're turning into an old woman in your declining years, Hitch. Ain't nothing out there but rocks and trees."

Faber shrugged and shucked his six-gun. "Have it your way." He reined around to face his men. "Anything happens, boys, just keep digging them spurs in them ponies." He reined back around. "Now, let's go."

High above, Cooper counted the number of riders.

Seventeen. He shook his head. "I reckon we could use a mite of luck here," he muttered to himself. At that moment, Luiz knelt beside the prone man and whispered urgently. "*El Patron*. The *caballo* the deputy leads—it belongs to Juan."

Cooper cursed softly. That meant that word had not reached the *hacienda*. Sheriff Faber and his gang of killers would hit the ranch without warning.

All Sam could do now was hope he could trim the number of riders enough to make a difference.

Despite his taunts to the sheriff, Bratcher rode with his Remington .44 in his hand, hammer cocked, finger on trigger, an act copied by every rider in the band.

Ominously, the bluff loomed ahead.

Lining the front blade sight of his Yellow Boy Henry on Faber, Cooper waited. Another two minutes, and Sheriff Faber would be shaking hands with Old Scratch. "Easy boys. Not yet. Let them get on in. They'll bunch up and can't turn around. They got to go on through then, and we'll have them like ducks on a pond for a quarter of a mile."

The only sounds in the crisp silence of the morning were the rhythmic clopping of iron shoes on rock.

A cruel grin played over Cooper's lips as his finger tightened slowly on the trigger. Taking care to allow for the downward angle, Cooper drew a deep breath and slowly released it.

Suddenly, the explosion of a percussion musket shattered the brittle silence of the morning.

Chapter Twenty-five

Cooper flinched, then cursed, and squeezed off a shot that sizzled past Faber's ear as the sheriff threw himself across the neck of his pony and sent the frightened animal racing down the road.

In the next few seconds, booming gunfire, obscene curses, and screams of pain bounced off the granite walls of the narrow canyon.

Desperately, Cooper tracked the fleeing sheriff with his front sight. Once, he thought he had Faber, but another rider suddenly raced between them, catching the slug and tumbling lifelessly from his saddle.

The barrel of the Henry was blistering hot by the time the firing pin fell on an empty chamber.

Three of Faber's men lay sprawled on the rocky road.

Cooper cursed. Only three! By all that was holy, only

three! He glanced around at his *vaqueros,* reminding himself of their limitations. Still, they had cut the number down to fourteen. And he has suffered no casualties. Except for Juan, he reminded himself bitterly.

Climbing stiffly to his feet, he gestured for his *vaqueros* to mount. He grabbed the pommel of his saddle. Just before he jerked himself into the saddle, a searing pain shot through his chest, doubling him over. He clenched his teeth, grimacing against the excruciating agony ripping through his chest.

"*El Patron!*" Luiz exclaimed, rushing to the old man.

Cooper shook his head, waving the alarmed *vaquero* away.

Several concerned *vaqueros* gathered around, staring at the old man helplessly.

After a few moments, Cooper straightened, his eyes closed, his hand on his chest, his clothes soaked with sweat. He drew several deep breaths. He looked around at his men. His weathered face was gaunt and wore a yellowish pall shiny with perspiration.

He reached, for the pommel again. Two *vaqueros* rushed to help him into the saddle. Cooper reined his pony around and headed out along the trail.

Luiz met the eyes of the two *vaqueros* and nodded to the old man. They understood. They would remain at his side.

They rode out, but within minutes, it was obvious the ride was too much for Sam. Luiz rode up beside the old man. "*El Patron*, you must rest. Let us make camp. I will send Rico and Jaime ahead to keep us informed of the sheriff. Besides, the sheriff is stronger, so we must be wiser."

Cooper stared dully at his ramrod several seconds. His eyes rolled up in his head, he fell to the side. Luiz caught him before he hit the ground.

While they laid Cooper on a blanket, Luiz called to one of the *vaqueros*. "Santo. Gather *el infierno taladra*. Make tea for *el Patron*."

With a brief nod, the *vaquero* disappeared into the forest searching for the hellbore, a winter blooming flower similar to a buttercup, containing properties to allay the pains of the heart, a remedy passed down through the generations from the Mayans.

Before Jaime and Rico rode out, Luiz whispered additional instructions. "One of you report back to us. The other must slip into the compound and hide. We must have the gates open when we arrive. *Comprende?*"

The two grinning young *vaqueros* nodded.

"Blast that old man," Faber muttered as he spurred his straining horse south along the winding road to the valley. Sam Cooper. That's the only jasper who would have dared pull such a stunt. As the gunshots faded behind him, Faber promised himself he would personally put a hole between the old man's eyes. He glanced over his shoulder. Three wild-eyed, riderless horses, their sweaty skin lathered white, raced after him.

When he felt confident he was beyond the reach of Sam, Sheriff Faber reined his pony down to a trot.

Bratcher pulled up beside him. "What in the Sam Hill was that all about, Faber? You didn't say nothing about us getting jumped."

Over the pounding of the horses' hooves, Faber barked. "What are you griping about? You're getting paid good American gold."

They rode past the empty sentry cabin and rounded a bend in the road. Ahead of them lay the valley, stretching five miles north to south and eight east to west.

Faber nodded to the *hacienda*. "Suck up your gut. That's where we're heading."

Perched on the northwest tower, the alert young *el chico* spotted the riders on the north road. The boy shaded his eyes against the noonday sun. With an excited yelp, he raced down the stone stairs and across the hardpan to the *hacienda*.

"*Señora* Inez, *Señora* Inez," he shouted as he burst through the back door into the *cocino*. "*Muchos vaqueros!*" He jabbed a skinny finger to the north road. "They come."

The matronly *señora* looked up from the pot of stew dangling from the pothook over the fire. She stared at the boy, gathering her thoughts, then waved her hand. "*Vamanos*. Tell the others. *Santa Maria*! I pray it is *el Patron*, but we take no chances. Go!"

Drying her hands on a heavy towel of spun cloth, she hurried into the salon. "Riders come."

Speck sat forward. "Who are they?

She shook her head. "I do not know."

Clint glanced at Speck. "Hard to say if our boys had time to get to Sam and bring him back so soon."

Speck knitted his brows. "Maybe they rode all night."

"Maybe. But, we're not taking any chances." Pushing to his feet, Clint grabbed the telescope off the dark mantel on the wall and quickly hurried to the northwest tower.

By now, the riders were almost a third of the way across the valley, riding hard. "Looks like a dozen or so," Clint muttered, peering through the telescope. Deftly, he adjusted it, bringing the fuzzy image into a crisp sharpness. He muttered a curse. "Faber!" He lowered the glass a moment, glaring across the valley, then placed it back to his eye. His lips moved as he counted. Finally, he lowered the glass. "Fourteen," he said, his cold eyes watching the riders.

Speck drawled. "Well, Partner. What are we waiting here for? Let's get our ponies and hightail it out of here while we can."

Back in the salon, *Señora* Inez waited expectantly.

Clint hurried through the *cocino*. "The law is coming. Send a boy to saddle our horses while we pack our plunder."

She nodded hurriedly. "*Sí.*"

As Clint and Speck rushed down the stairs to the storeroom with their gear slung over their shoulders, *Señora* Inez burst from the secret panel beneath the stairs. She looked up at them, her eyes wide and her face contorted with distress. "*Señor Cleve*. The horses.

They are dead. Some *diablo* cut their throats and killed the *cucaracha*, Chochiti."

Clint muttered a curse. "Bodine!" He spun. "Quick, the stable."

Moments later, they rushed into the stable with the *señora* on their heels. She called out to her husband. "Diego. Two horses. The best we have."

Two *vaqueros* grabbed hair ropes from the pegs on the wall and quickly built loops and deftly snaked them through the air, dabbing them gently over the heads of two deep-chested sorrels.

While the *vaqueros* fit bridles and bits, others slapped on saddles.

Speck's arm was stiffening, so one of the *vaqueros* tied his bedroll behind the cantle. "I don't like it, Clint," Speck said with a grimace. "It's bad luck to use another jasper's saddle."

Swinging aboard his sorrel, Clint replied. "You ain't got no choice now. You sure can't outrun Faber on foot."

"Reckon not." Using his good arm, Speck hauled himself into the saddle. "Let's ride."

They burst from the stable door and headed for the river, hoping to keep the *hacienda* between them and the sheriff. Once at the river, they would cut back north and lose themselves in the thick forest surrounding the valley.

Clint threw a hasty glance over his shoulder. Speck grinned. "Don't slow down, partner," the lanky cowpoke shouted over the pounding of hooves. "I'll run up your back if you do."

As soon as the two raced from the stable, the *señora* and her husband returned to the tunnel where they dragged the body of Chochiti to the river and dumped it in.

Clint urged his pony faster. When he and Speck were less than a hundred yards from the river, Faber rounded the corner of the compound.

"There they go," shouted the sheriff, digging his spurs into his horse and shucking his six-gun.

Clint dropped low over his pony's neck as a barrage of gunfire exploded behind him. Slugs tore up chunks of soggy earth around the hooves of his horse.

Moments later, the two dropped down the slope to the river and out of sight of the sheriff's hired killers. Leaning to his left, Clint turned the straining sorrel north into the protection of the narrow strip of trees along the riverbank, heading for the welcome sanctuary of the forest two miles distant. Yet he knew they would not be safe until they reached the rocky soil of the foothills where they could hide their trail, which was obvious in the muddy shoreline.

He glanced back. Speck's eyes were closed, his teeth clenched as he slapped his horse's hindquarters with the reins in a desperate effort to urge his pony to run even faster. The bandage on his left arm was stained bright red with fresh blood.

Around the next bend in the river, they ran into a herd of long-haired mustangs milling about at the river's edge. The herd exploded in every direction, sending a rush of hope surging through Clint's veins. There would be tracks everywhere. Just beyond the riverbank was a thick growth of vines and briars covering an ancient windfall.

He jerked his pony up the riverbank and reined up behind the windfall. Speck pulled up beside him. Clint shucked his six-gun and waited, his breath coming in labored gasps.

Moments later came the pounding of hooves. Clint held his breath, and as the riders passed, he slowly released it. When the sound of hoofbeats faded to the north, he muttered, "Well, partner—looks like we dodged the lead plum this time." Wearing a crooked grin, he looked around at Speck and froze.

Speck was slouched forward, his hand clutching the pommel of his saddle. Sweat dripped from his pale face.

Clint grabbed his arm. "Speck! Speck! What happened?"

The lanky cowpoke's eyes slowly opened. He forced a faint grin. "I knew I ought'n to use another jasper's saddle." He coughed, and fresh, red blood bubbled from his lips. "I shouldn't not done it."

His eyes drifted closed, and he tumbled to the ground.

Chapter Twenty-six

Clint dropped to his knees and slipped his arm around Speck's back, cradling his head in the crook of his arm. He glanced at his own hand, which was covered with his partner's blood. "Speck! Speck! Hold on. You hear me. Hold on."

His pale face beaded with sweat, the freckle-faced cowboy opened his eyes slightly. "O—one thing I hate about leaving all this—" he coughed, wincing at the pain.

Tears blurred Clint's eyes. "You're not leaving nothing, Speck. You hear me? Just hold on. He swallowed hard, trying to wash away the rawness in his throat. "It's my turn to take care of you, you hear?"

The slight cowpoke mumbled. "Amy." A broken chuckle came from his bloody lips. "Amy. You know, I never had no family." He forced another laugh followed by a wracking cough. "Just my luck. Now—now it don't appear I'll never have the chance."

"You will. I promise you that chance. Just don't quit on me, blast you. Don't quit."

Speck's eyes drifted shut. He mumbled. Clint bent closer to listen. "Watch yourself, Clint. I ain't going to be around to look—" his breath caught, and then he gasped, "—after you no more." His sunken chest rose and fell. Each cycle took a few seconds longer and was not as pronounced as the previous until finally, there was no movement at all.

Clint lost track of the time he knelt in the mud holding his partner of eight years, eight years that had brought them closer than brothers, eight years of sharing dreams and wishes, eight years building new lives.

"You know, Speck," Clint muttered in a hoarse whisper. "I don't even know where you come from. I just woke up that day in Valverde, and you was tending my carved-up carcass." He shook his head. "I don't even know who to notify."

Distant voices along the riverbank cut into his grieving. He glanced up, numbed by his partner's death. But as the voices grew closer, a spark of anger ignited in his chest, quickly burning away at his numbed senses until a searing rage roared in his ears like a firestorm sweeping up the mountain slopes.

Through the tangle of undergrowth, he saw four riders heading in his direction in a slow trot. They were hard and grizzled, the kind who would kill their own kin if the price was high enough.

Gently, he laid Speck back on the ground, then rose to his feet. He wiped his bloody hand on his pants, slipped his .36s from the holsters, spun the cylinders that purred like newborn kittens, dropped them back in their holsters, and stepped from behind the windfall.

He halted beside a tall pine, his arms hanging loosely at his side. Through cold eyes, he watched the four riders draw closer. Immersed in their own conversation, they failed to notice Clint until they were less than thirty feet from him.

"Hey, look!" one exclaimed, reining up and staring at Clint. For a moment, a flash of surprise lit their hard faces, then faded into cold determination.

The others reined up. One glanced around, then growled. "You Bollinger?"

"That's right, boys, and you're going to meet your maker." Even before his words faded away, his six-guns magically appeared in his hands, belching death. Before any of the four could move a muscle, three lay dead or dying on the muddy ground.

Clint centered the muzzles on the fourth hired killer. "Tell Faber I'm coming."

The gunnie studied Clint several moments, a touch of amusement in his eyes and a faint grin on his rugged face. "I'll tell him, Bollinger." He gave his head a brief shake. "You got guts. I hand you that, but you ain't got a chance. Were I you, I'd make myself invisible in this neck of the woods."

After the gunman rode on leaving his compadres lying in the mud, Clint loaded Speck on his pony and made his way into the High Lonesome, the slopes of Eagle Peak where the snow lay thick and heavy.

Gently wrapping his partner in his bedroll tarp, Clint dug out a drift of snow beneath a small upthrust of granite and laid him to rest. After stacking rocks over him, Clint covered the grave with snow. When he finished, he stepped back and wiped at the perspiration on his forehead. "Don't worry, Speck. I'll be back. You'll have a proper funeral and a proper grave down in the valley there—where you'll always have a family to look after you."

A cold, silent night fell across the mountain as Clint stood without moving, staring down at where his partner lay.

Bratcher listened as his man related the events of the afternoon to the sheriff. Faber glared at the cowpoke. "Bollinger's bluffing. He ain't stupid enough to take on eleven of us."

With a wry grin playing over his lips, the hired gun shrugged. "He ain't stupid, Sheriff. But, he means it. I faced enough gunnies in my life to know when one means it. He's one of them, and he's fast. I never saw him grab them hoglegs of his. And Chase and them other two gunnies was knocked out of the saddles before they could spit. If I ever seen me a rogue wolf, that jasper is it."

Faber studied the hardcase a moment. "You scared of him, Utah?"

Utah pursed his lips. After a moment, he nodded. "Yep, but I figure that might give me the edge I need."

The sheriff snorted and poured a glass of tequila. "So, he's fast, but I still say he's bluffing. He won't come here."

Bratcher spoke up, a hint of respect in his voice. "If Utah says the jasper's coming, Faber, he's coming."

The sheriff turned his angry eyes on Bratcher who wore a taunting smile. He studied the smiling killer. Maybe he was right. That being the case, maybe there was some way to turn that little piece of information to their advantage.

He glanced at Zeke. "Didn't you say that Bollinger and the old man were kin?"

"That's what that Mex cook said."

Faber grunted. "Get her in here."

Moments later, *Señor* Inez shuffled fearfully into the room. When Faber put the question to her, she glanced at Zeke, then nodded. "*Si. El Patron*, he take *Señor* Cleve in when he was just a boy."

Faber waved her away, and the *señora* scurried back into the kitchen, pausing in the shadows just around the doorjamb to listen.

The sheriff nodded slowly. "All right. So Bollinger claims he's coming after us. If we fiddlefoot around and drag out the search for him, he might get one or two of us, but, we ain't going to do that. We're going to make him come to us on our terms."

Puzzled, Bratcher glanced at Zeke, then frowned at Faber. "How do you reckon on doing that?"

The sheriff stroked his chin with his thumb and fingers. "I ain't quite sure, but it'll come to me."

In the *cocino*, *Señora* Inez pressed her work-worn fingers to her lips. Her flashing black eyes studied the spacious kitchen. A sly smile played over her lips. Quickly, she slid trays of corn bread into the rock ovens. She turned to her two helpers and pulled a large platter from a shelf. "*Pronto. Mucho papadzules*. This many," she said, holding her hand six inches over the platter.

The women nodded and the *señora* scurried from the *hacienda* to her small dwelling near the stables where all the servants lived.

She called her husband and the other servants from the stable. She told them of what she had overheard. "We must send *los ninos* through the tunnel to the cave north of the valley."

Diego, her husband, frowned. "Why should we do such?"

She shook her head in frustration at his slow wit. "Remember what the one called Turner did with our *nina*, Damita? He use her to make me speak of *Señor* Cleve, the act of a coward. Who is to say the sheriff would not do the same to make *Señor* Cleve come in to them?"

For a few moments, the peons discussed the situation among themselves, then nodded. "We go."

She glanced out the stable door. "Soon, it will be dark. We must move quickly, but not so quickly as to make the gringos suspicious. Diego, you go with Damita and the *ninos* of Jose and Vincentes. Then the *ninos* of Galeno and Nicanor. Take them to the cave. I go back to the *cocino* now. Do not enter until I say. And make certain the little ones remain silent."

Nicanor frowned. "The gringos will be angry when they learn the *ninos* have left. What will they do to us?"

Her eyes grew hard. "As long as my Damita is safe, I do not care."

Nodding quickly, the peons hurried to their tiny dwellings.

By the time *Señora* Inez returned to the *hacienda*, the sun had set behind the mountain peaks and cold shadows had spread over the valley. She pulled out the trays of hot corn bread and tossed a few more peppers in the black *frijole* and pork stew. She opened a bag and pulled out a handful of *epazote*, an herb that countered the effect of black beans. She hesitated, then with a devious smile, replaced the handful of herb in the bag. Let the *gringos* suffer.

Several men sat about the salon, enjoying tequila in front of the newly repaired fireplace.

Faber shouted. "Hey, *señoritas,* bring us something to eat. We're hungry."

Moments later, bowls brimming with steaming black *frijole* and pork stew and platters of hot corn bread were placed on the table along with half-a-dozen unopened bottles of tequila. A platter of *papadzules*, rolled tortillas stuffed with fatty pork, was set in the middle of the table. On either side was a bowl of spicy pumpkin seed sauce, deliberately made a little more spicy by the *señora*.

Faber's men jostled each other for a place at the table. Busy poking grub down their gullets, they failed to notice the shadowy figures slipping in the back door of the kitchen and down into the storeroom.

Señora Inez and the other kitchen workers hovered over the owlhoots at the table, refilling their bowls with thick chunks of pork and their glasses with tequila while keeping furtive eyes on the children ghosting through the kitchen.

By the time the last of the children had disappeared into the storeroom, Faber's men were only half finished with the huge repast.

Zeke unsteadily turned up his glass to wash down the last mouthful of corn bread. Suddenly, he paused, a vague idea tumbling through his alcohol soaked brain. He tried to concentrate, to stop the thought from spinning. Slowly, he managed to focus on the tenuous recollection. He nodded. "That's it. That's how we'll draw Bollinger to us," he muttered, his words slurred.

He jerked his head around and glanced down the table at Sheriff Faber who by now was growing glassy-eyed and loud. "Sheriff!" He shook his head, trying to form the words with his thick tongue. "You come up with an idea on Bollinger?"

Faber shook his head. "I'm working on it." He elbowed Deputy Scruggs who was sitting at his side. "We're working on it, ain't that right, deputy?"

Scruggs laughed drunkenly. "Yeah, Sheriff." He held up his half full glass. "We're sure working on it." He broke into a spasm of laughter at his joke.

The sheriff blinked his eyes, trying to focus on Zeke the end of the table. "Why?"

Zeke set his glass on the table and shook his head, trying to remember what he had planned to say, but the thought had vanished into the drunken recesses of his brain. He shook his head. "Don't know. Just wondering, that's all. Just wondering."

Chapter Twenty-seven

Clint stared woodenly at Speck's grave. The raw-boned cowpoke had spent the night squatting against an ancient pine, a wool blanket about his shoulders his only concession to the bitter cold.

He blinked his red-rimmed eyes and slowly struggled to his feet, stretching his cold-stiffened muscles. His sorrel stood tied to a tree limb, staring at him. As if in a trance, Clint built a small fire to boil some coffee. He had no taste for the thick liquid nor any desire for food this morning, but the pragmatist in him knew that he had to have sustenance in his belly if he were to carry out his plans.

He forced himself to down a breakfast that tasted like dried cow patties and hog wallow water.

As he sat staring into the fire, he remembered Speck's caution. "You got to be careful, Clint. Word gets out that

Bollinger ain't dead, and you and me got big problems."

Clint hadn't laughed at his partner's concern. Speck was right, and the rawboned cowpoke knew it. For eight years, Cleve Bollinger had been dead to the world, dead to the law, and dead to all the young gunnies anxious to make a name for themselves. Clint sighed with resignation and poured the dregs of his coffee on the small fire. Now it don't much matter, he told himself.

His eyes grew cold and his heart hard with resolve. One way or another, by this time next week, Faber and Rawlings would be shaking hands with old scratch in front of the fires of hades. And if it happened that he was right alongside them, it wouldn't make much difference.

Luiz and two *vaqueros* stood silently studying Sam who had finally dropped into a peaceful slumber. "The tea of *el infierno taladra* did much good for *el Patron*. We let him sleep. The valley is but a few hours." A flake of snow touched his cheek. He looked up into the gray skies as another flake of snow brushed his swarthy cheek. He grimaced. "Perhaps we should move. The clouds are heavy and thick. There might be much snow."

One of the *vaqueros* protested. "But what of *el Patron?* Does he have the strength?"

Luiz gave him a wry grin. "*Si. El Patron* has much strength when it comes to his children."

Fifteen minutes later, the small band rode out with Luiz at the side of Sam.

Having fallen into his bunk fully dressed the night before, Zeke awakened with a vile taste in his mouth. Sitting up on the edge of his bunk, he reached for the almost empty bottle of tequila lying on its side on the floor. He turned it up and drained it, then rose unsteadily and grabbed his hat.

He stepped outside into the bracing cold and crossed the hardpan to the horse trough where he broke the ice and splashed the frigid water on his face. He shivered, and then his mouth began watering as the rich aroma of fried pork and hot coffee drifted through the frosty air.

Zeke had lost count of the number of times he had awakened with a hangover until finally, while he would still become intoxicated, his system had adjusted itself so that he never awakened with a headache or a queasy stomach, just an overpowering sense of lassitude.

During the night, clouds had moved in and light flakes of snow began drifting down.

In the salon, Sheriff Faber with his two deputies was putting away platefuls of pork, tortillas, potatoes, and washing it down with steaming coffee.

As soon as Zeke saw the sheriff, he remembered his idea from the night before. He slid in at the table. "Sheriff, I come up with a thought that might help."

Faber looked up and arched an eyebrow. "What might that be?" He asked with a mouthful of food bulging his cheeks.

Turner hesitated as one of the kitchen *señoras* slid a heaping platter of pork and potatoes in front of him. After she left, he leaned forward and whispered. "Bollinger is Cooper's adopted son. Some of the greasers, the old ones, they been with Cooper for years. Bollinger knows them. All we have to do is get word to him that if he don't give hisself up, we'll shoot one of the Mexican kids. One every hour until he comes in." He snorted. "There's too many of them dirty little brats running around nohow."

Faber looked up from his plate. He stared at Zeke curiously, and then at his deputies. A cruel grin twisted his thick lips. "It beats sitting around here."

Zeke laughed. "And I know which kid to start with." He turned to the *cocino. Señora, Señora!*"

Señora Inez hurried from the kitchen. She halted and waited, saying nothing. Zeke growled. "Bring me that choice little daughter of yours, *pronto!*"

The *señora* closed her eyes and tried to still her trembling muscles. She opened her eyes and looked squarely at Turner. "She is not here. I sent her away." She hesitated, then added. "We send all the *ninos* away."

For several moments, Turner and Faber stared at her, unable to grasp the meaning of her words. Finally, Faber spoke up. "What did you say?" Before she could reply, he continued. "Sent them where and why?"

The frightened, but determined *señora* stared hard at Faber. "Away, so you cannot hurt them, *Señor.*"

Suddenly, Zeke understood what the woman had done. With a roar of rage, he leaped to his feet and slammed the muzzle of his six-gun across her face, spinning her around and slamming her to the flagstone floor.

Moaning softly, she lay still, blood spreading in a pool about her head.

Two kitchen helpers rushed in to her aid, then stopped, staring at the *gringos* in fear.

Faber nodded to the supine woman and gestured for the women to take her away. As they dragged her from the room, he looked up at Turner who was still on his feet. "She ain't going to do us no good now."

Turner jammed his revolver back in its holster and sneered. "Think not? Just watch. I know what to do."

Faber frowned. "Yeah? And just what is that?"

Pot-bellied Scruggs grunted. "Blazes, Sheriff. Muddy as it is out there, we can track them kids."

With a disgusted shake of his head, the sheriff replied. "That's what Bollinger wants, to get us out there where he can pick us off one at a time."

"I told you, Sheriff," said Turner. "I can get Bollinger in here."

"They ain't going to tell you nothing about the kids. I know the kind. They might be dumb and stupid, but they take care of their blasted kids. Beat'em all you want, and they still ain't going to talk. All you'll hear is *no hablo ingles, no hablo ingles.*"

With a grunt, Turner called one of the women from the kitchen and sent her to fetch the hands from the stable. When the stable hands returned, they stood, hats in hand, in front of Turner, heads bowed.

Turner growled, "Any of you greasers know where them kids went?"

They looked at each other dumbly and shook their heads.

Turner chuckled. "Didn't figure you did." He looked at the first one. "*Nombre?* What are you called?"

"Galeno, *Señor*," the slight Mexican replied.

"How long you lived here at the *hacienda?*"

With a slight shrug, he replied, "Three, maybe four years, *Señor*."

Turner glanced at the kitchen. "The *señora?* Inez? She's been here a long time, ain't she?"

"Many years, *Señor*"

Faber grunted. "What are you getting at, Turner?"

A sly grin played over Zeke's bearded face. "You'll see."

The broad-shouldered killer nodded to Dowd and Scruggs. "Work this greaser over. Don't kill him, just mark him up good. I want him to be able to ride."

"Huh?" Confused by the order, Dowd glanced at Faber.

The sheriff frowned, then nodded for Dowd to do what Turner said.

With a leering grin, Dowd knocked the small Mexican to the floor. Scruggs joined the fun, and between the two of them, they worked Galeno over until the hapless stable hand's face looked like it had been caught in a stampede.

Turner stepped in. "That's enough." He grabbed the battered man by the front of his blood-splattered blouse and jerked him to his feet. "You get out there and find Bollinger. You tell him that if he don't come in here today, we'll send the *señora* out tomorrow, draped belly down over a saddle. *Comprende?*"

Galeno stood, his shoulders slumped, his head down, and faced Turner.

Impatiently, Turner slapped him. "I said do you *comprende?*"

"*Si.*" Galeno managed to whisper through swollen lips.

With a smug smirk, Turner barked at the other stable hands, "Put him on a good horse and get him out of here, *pronto!*"

After the stable hands put the battered *vaquero* in the saddle, Jose asked, "Where will you go?"

One eye swollen shut, Galeno peered down. "I go see Diego. Perhaps he knows of the one named Bollinger."

The light snowfall dusted the shoulders of Clint's woolen Mackinaw coat as he made his way down the foothills. Although he didn't figure any of Faber's men would be out so early, he still moved with the wary alertness and cold determination of a mountain lion stalking its prey, pausing frequently to study the forest around and behind him.

He still wasn't certain just how he was going to get to the sheriff, but he knew that if Faber was gone, his hired killers would scatter like quail.

There was always the dynamite stored in the cave

high above the timberline in the western mountains. His eyes narrowed. The dynamite was a last resort, but one to which he would turn to rid the world of trash like Sheriff Faber.

"Best thing for the time being, Clint," he muttered. "Is to see just what comes your way. Then go whole hog."

As the valley came in sight, Clint cut back toward the river. Thirty minutes later, he picked up a whiff of wood smoke on the currents of the air swirling about in the foothills. He reined up beside an ancient white fir on the crest of a gentle slope.

He caught the smell again. Instinctively, he flipped the leather loop off the .36 on his right hip and rode warily toward the source of the wood smoke.

Fifteen minutes later, he reined up on a rounded ridge of basaltic rock covered with a light cover of snow. The pungent smell of wood smoke was stronger. He heard a snort above him and jerked around in time to see a large mule deer spin and vanish into the forest above.

Then a distant voice drifted through the thin air. He looked around. On the next ridge, he spotted a small boy in the mouth of a large cave. The boy spun around as if someone had called to him and disappeared back into the cave.

Clint rode up above the cave and dismounted. Carefully, he descended the snow-covered rocks. Colt in hand, he paused just outside the mouth of the cave and listened.

From inside came the soft chatter of children interspersed with the voice of a man. What in the Sam Hill was a bunch of kids doing out here?

The hair on the back of his neck bristled with ominous foreboding. Flexing his fingers about the butt of his .36, he slipped around the corner of the mouth. To his surprise, he recognized Diego, husband to *Señora* Inez.

"Diego!"

The children screamed in terror at his voice, but Diego calmed them. "*Tenga no temor, los niños.* Have no fear, children. He is a friend. Do not be afraid."

Quickly Diego told Clint of the events at the *hacienda*. With bravado, he added, "I want to stay and fight, but *Señora*, she tell me to take the children so the sheriff not hurt them."

Clenching his fist, Clint turned his cold eyes in the direction of the *hacienda*. He remembered *Señora* Inez telling him Zeke threatened Damita. And now the sidewinder was trying the same play once again.

But, if the children were not there to use as hostages, then what would Turner and Faber do next?

Chapter Twenty-eight

A ragged voice behind Clint answered his question. "Diego!"

"*Mi dios!*" Diego exclaimed when he saw the swollen and bruised face of Galeno.

Clint rushed to help the battered *vaquero* from his saddle.

As Diego bathed the stable hand's face, Galeno gave Clint the message from the sheriff.

"The *señora*?" Clint asked, his eyes narrowing with cold fury.

Galeno nodded and drew a finger diagonally across his face. "Turner, he hit her with his gun. He will kill her if you do not go to the *hacienda* before night."

Diego leaped to his feet. "I will go."

"No." Galeno shook his head. "They say Bollinger."

The chill of death settled in Clint's chest, filling him

with a terrible resignation. He had no choice. He must do as the sheriff demanded, but if he could take Turner and Faber with him, then he'd settle for whatever awaited him afterward, the law or hades.

Clint studied the small fire, from time to time glancing at the children who were watching him with a mixture of curiosity and fear.

Diego spoke. "You know they will kill you, *Señor* Cleve."

Clint rose to his feet. "I reckon there'll be a heap of killing, old friend. If killing is what it takes to get this place back for the old man, then I'll be satisfied."

Faber stood in front of the fire, rubbing his hands together. Dowd sat at the table and poured a glass of tequila. "Quiet around here, Sheriff. Not much going on. I ain't seen more than two or three of the Mexs around."

"Can't blame them," Faber snorted. "Blasted snow. I'd stay in my bed too if I had a sweet young thing to keep me warm." He leered at Dowd. "Fact is, I been thinking about finding me one around here."

Dowd laughed, but the fact he had seen so few *vaqueros* and kitchen help in the last few hours still bothered him. He glanced into the kitchen. *Señora* Inez, her nose swollen and both eyes black, shuffled slowly around the great table to tend the pot over the fire.

"You think Bollinger will come in?"

"Yeah." Faber continued to rub his hands in front of the fire. "He'll come in. You can bank on it."

Outside at the watchtower on the northwest corner, a shivering cowpoke peered into the increasing snowfall. His teeth chattered as he beat on his arms to warm himself. Finally, he muttered a curse. "It's too cold out here. Faber can get someone else to stand up here and watch the blasted snow fall."

The snow continued to fall as Cooper and his *vaqueros* rode down the last mountain slope before reaching the valley. "There she be," Cooper shouted above the pounding of hooves.

Luiz nodded, studying the old man, trying to gauge his endurance. His breathing was hard, but the fire in his old eyes told the ramrod that Cooper was handling the stress of the hard ride well.

He focused his eyes on the *hacienda* in the middle of the valley. Neither of the young *vaqueros* he had sent out had returned. He hoped that at least one of them had managed to slip in and hide. If they were to surprise the gringos as *el Patron* hoped, the gates must be open and remain open. If their force was trapped within the compound, the superior firepower of the *gringos* would overpower them.

The front door opened and a gust of icy wind swept in, blowing snow into the salon. Bratcher slammed the door behind him. "Something's going on, Faber."

The sheriff frowned at him and reached for the tequila and a glass. "What do you mean?"

Bratcher nodded to the stables. "The horses ain't

been fed, and I can't find a single *vaquero* anywheres around."

Turner spoke up. "Now that you mention it, I didn't see none around either."

Faber paused in the middle of filling his glass. "They're probably in their shacks, staying out of the weather."

"Nope. Ain't there either. The shacks is empty."

Dowd spoke up. "I told you, Sheriff. It was too quiet around here."

Faber glanced into the kitchen as the *señora* went about her job. Come to think of it, he hadn't seen the other two kitchen helpers for a spell. He set his glass down and strode into the kitchen.

Señora Inez didn't look up. She continued measuring corn meal for the tortillas.

"Hey, Mex! Where are the other women who work here?"

Pausing, she kept her eyes lowered. "I do not know, *Señor*. I think maybe they went to their homes after breakfast, but I do not know."

The burly sheriff grabbed her arm and spun her to face him. "You're a lying Mexican *la puta*!" He raised his hand to deliver a slap.

She stared up at him, and he could see from the determination in her eyes that no amount of punishment would make her speak. Over his shoulder, he called out. "Dowd. You and Scruggs search the entire compound. Bring every greaser you find to me. Bratcher. Send some of your boys to help." He grabbed *Señora* by the arm and dragged her to the salon where he threw her into a chair. "Don't get out of that chair or you're a dead Mexican, *comprende?*"

Señora Inez simply glared at him.

In the kitchen, a pair of dark eyes peered through the crack between the doorjamb and the storeroom door. Silently, the door closed, and Nicanor hurried out the tunnel.

Ten minutes later, Dowd and Scruggs returned, followed by a handful of Bratcher's hired guns. "Ain't a single greaser to be found, Sheriff," said Dowd.

Faber glared at him. "Did you search everywhere, every room in this house?"

Scruggs nodded. "Yes sir, Sheriff. We searched the top floor, this floor, and the storehouse below the kitchen. "Nary a sign of any Mex."

The sheriff glanced at *Señora* Inez. He thought he saw a flicker of a smile on her bruised face, but he wasn't certain. He narrowed his eyes. "You know where they all done gone to." He pulled out his revolver and cocked it. "Tell me where, or I'll kill you." He extended his arm, lining the front blade on her forehead.

Riding along the riverbank to the tunnel, Clint passed three mounds of snow, the three jaspers he had gunned down the day before.

He quickly discarded the idea of riding in from the valley where he could be easily spotted. To get to Faber and Turner, he had to slip in before they knew he was around. That meant the tunnel. And whoever had slit the horses' throats would be watching.

A few minutes later, he spotted several Mexican peons running up the river in his direction. "What the?" he muttered, reining up.

The first peon who spotted Clint threw up his arms and begged for mercy. Clint spoke to him rapidly in his own tongue, explaining who he was, assuring the cowering man that he was safe.

Then the stable hand, Jose, stepped forward and faced those behind him. "*Amigos*! Do not fear. This is the son of *el Patron*. I see him when he ride into *hacienda*."

When Clint asked why they were leaving the *hacienda*, Jose explained. "*Señora* Inez tell us to run. The men at the *hacienda* would kill us, she say. We go to cave with our children."

Clint glanced downriver, but there were no more figures heading toward them. "Where is the *Señora*?"

Jose frowned. "She stay behind, *Señor*. She say she will soon come."

At that moment, another figure appeared on the riverbank near the mouth of the tunnel. Jose grinned. "There she is."

Clint studied the figure, which was too far to identify, but from the way the figure was running, it was a man, not a woman. With a click of his tongue, he rode to meet the man.

It was Nicanor. "They keep her prisoner, in the salon," he said. "The sheriff was much angry when he learn everyone gone." He paused, then asked, "You go to bring the *Señora* away, *Señor?*"

With a brief nod, Clint replied. "I'll try. How did you get out, the tunnel?"

Nicanor grinned. "*Si.* They not watch tunnel, *Señor.*"

Clint nodded, hoping the peon was right.

In the hacienda, a faint smile played over *Señora* Inez'*s* swollen lips. "I do not think you will shoot me, *Señor*. If you do, you will not learn what you ask, nor will the one you call Bollinger have reason to come here."

Faber's face darkened in anger. His finger tightened on the trigger.

Bratcher laughed. "Hold on, Sheriff. Like it or not, she's right. She's the only hole card we got if we want Bollinger to come to us. Kill her, and then that means we've got to get out there and traipse through a foot of snow in the valley and ten foot snowdrifts in the mountains."

For several long seconds, Sheriff Faber remained unmoving, the muzzle still centered on the *señora's* forehead. Finally, he drew a breath and lowered the six-gun. "You're right," he growled, still glaring at the small woman who matched the fire in his eyes with a blazing inferno in her own.

"But if he don't show up," he said to her. "Come nightfall, I'll kill you."

Grimacing as he passed the two dead horses, Clint made his way through the tunnel into the storeroom.

With his ear to the door, he heard voices on the other side in the kitchen.

Easing the door open slightly, he peered into the salon. He recognized Sheriff Faber among the several hombres milling about in front of the fire. He stiffened when he heard the name, Bratcher, a name known throughout the territory that was the embodiment of cruelty and terror. And word had drifted down to the saloons in Tucson that the killer was fast, faster than the dead gunfighter, Cleve Bollinger.

From the movement and talk from the salon, Clint guessed the number of men to be maybe half-a-dozen. As long as Turner and Faber are there, he told himself, palming his .36s and easing the door open.

He figured he could take four and the other two would put lead in him. A calculated gamble. More than once, he had made it carrying lead slugs, but that was years ago, and he was ten years younger then.

Slipping into the shadows of the *cocina*, he crouched behind the great table in the middle of the floor, peering through the legs into the salon. He spotted Faber, slouched in a heavy chair, nursing a glass of tequila.

Moments later, a thin man wearing a leather vest poured himself a drink. From the conversation, Clint learned the slender man was Bratcher. All that was left was Zeke.

Faber's voice echoed from the salon. "Dowd. Go call the boys in here. I got me an idea. Find Turner too."

Clint couldn't afford to hold off until more men arrived. Turner would have to wait.

He rose silently and stepped from the darkness into the doorway, noting with relief there were only four jaspers in the room.

Stifling a gasp of surprise, *Señora* Inez saw him immediately, but the others failed to see him for several seconds. Then Faber spotted him. "What the—Bollinger!"

As one, the other three spun to face him, their hands poised above the butts of their revolvers.

Clint glared at the sheriff. "Your string has run out, Sheriff. Yours too, Bratcher."

Dowd licked his lips, his eyes wide with fear.

Bratcher snorted. "You ain't going up against the four of us. You'd catch enough lead to sink a Yankee clipper."

"You'll sink right along with me." Clint crouched lower. "Anytime you're ready."

Suddenly, a muzzle jabbed him in the back. "Say good-bye, Bollinger!"

Chapter Twenty-nine

Clint froze.

A leering grin contorted Faber's square face. "About time you showed up, Turner."

At that moment, the boarded up glass door burst open and a lanky cowpoke with a week-old beard raced in. "Bratcher! It's Cooper. Th—"

He pitched forward on his face and then came the report of a rifle.

In the next instant, a salvo of gunfire ripped the remaining glass door to shreds and tore chunks out of the board covering the other door.

Clint threw himself backward and spun, swinging his left arm behind his back to knock Turner's hand aside. At the same time, he shucked his .36 and as he came face to face with Turner, jammed it in the killer's belly and pulled the trigger.

The force of Clint's lunge sent him stumbling to the kitchen floor. He rolled over and touched off two more slugs, knocking Turner backward through the doorway into the salon and tumbling into the fireplace.

Turner lay in the fire a moment, then screamed and lurched forward, staggering into the kitchen and sprawling face down on the floor.

Quickly, Clint rolled behind the heavy table, peering into the smoke-filled salon as the fight continued. From outside, slugs slammed into the stone wall, ricocheting in every direction. The salon reverberated with the steady fire Faber and Bratcher were returning.

The acrid stench of gunsmoke began to fill the room.

Rising into a crouch, Clint eased along the wall to the doorway, trying to find an angle where he could see into the salon. He eased forward another step, craning his neck.

Suddenly, a six-gun boomed and a chunk of wall inches from his head exploded. Clint jerked back, squinting into the thickening smoke.

"It's Bollinger," Bratcher yelled. "Turner didn't get him."

"Get him, blast it, get him," Faber shouted above the din of gunfire.

"Poke," Bratcher shouted at one of his men. "Get over in the corner behind the couch "You can get a clean shot at Bollinger from there."

Clint knew the instant he stuck his head in the door, he'd catch a lead plum between the eyes. He glanced over his shoulder into the darkened kitchen. His eyes fell on the body of Zeke lying in the shadows. An idea came to him.

He pulled Zeke around so his feet faced the door and his body was half in the shadows and half out. Then he crept to the side of the door. After a moment, he stuck his hand around the jamb and threw off a single shot toward the couch.

Immediately, two six-guns boomed from behind the couch.

Clint groaned loudly, then silently glided into the dark shadows in the corner of the kitchen.

"We hit him," a voice shouted, one Clint recognized as the deputy, Dowd.

"Find out, but watch your step. He's sneakier than a rattlesnake. And a heap more dangerous," Faber shouted.

A frightened voice cried out, "I ain't going back there."

Bratcher's guttural voice replied, "You will or I'll kill you, Poke."

Outside, Cooper's small band continued to rake the *hacienda* with gunfire. From time to time above the roar of gunfire came a scream of pain or a shout of triumph.

Clint crouched lower in the shadows, his muscles tense and sweat stinging his eyes despite the frigid weather outside.

Keeping his eyes fixed on the smoke-filled doorway, he deftly replaced the Colt cylinder with a fully loaded one.

The gunfire seemed to be losing its intensity outside.

Suddenly a shadow appeared and crouched beside the jamb. Moments later, a second shadow joined the first.

Flexing his fingers on the butt of his six-gun, Clint, scarcely breathing, waited for a better shot.

A hushed voice drifted through the shadows. "There he is, on the floor."

Dowd muttered, "You sure he's dead?"

A plume of yellow cut through the smoke and the boom of the six-gun echoed off the thick rock walls of the kitchen. Turner's body jerked.

"If he wasn't, he is now," Poke muttered with a touch of bravado.

Slowly, the two rose to their feet and eased toward the body. As they drew nearer, Dowd looked around. "Hey, what happened to Zeke. I don't see him nowhere."

Clint rose, his .36 cocked and leveled at the two shadowy figures. "Sure you do, boys. He's right at your feet."

Both men tried to spin around, but Clint's .36 belched flame six times in what appeared to be a single explosion of yellow fire, knocking Dowd over the table and sending the Poke stumbling back through the doorway.

Clint holstered the empty six-gun and shucked his second. Now it was Faber and Bratcher's time.

At the doorway, he pressed up against the wall. The gunfire became sporadic.

Suddenly, a shout from outside broke through the now intermittent firing. "They flee, *el Patron,* they flee."

At that moment footsteps sounded on the hard tile in

the adjacent room and in the next instant, *Señora* Inez exclaimed joyfully, "*El Patron! El Patron!* You are here. *Mi Dios*, we have been blessed by *la Madre Santa*."

Sam Cooper's cracked voice called out. "Inez! Are you hurt?"

She ignored his question. "*Pronto, el Patron. Señor* Cleve. He is hurt."

With a relieved grin on his face, Clint stepped into the salon, smoking six-gun still in hand. "You're wrong there, *Señora*." He holstered his .36 and his grin grew wider as he looked at Cooper. "I'm mighty glad to see you."

Cooper stared at him a moment, then limped across the room and threw his arms about Clint's shoulders. "Reckon I grew a few brains, son. After all," he added, backing away and winking up at Clint. "You ain't the only one what's done stupid things."

A strange sense of contentment came over Clint. For the first time since he had returned, the old man had called him 'son.' He nodded. "Reckon not—pa."

Cooper glanced in the kitchen. "Where's your pard, Speck?"

The smile faded from the rawboned man's rugged face. His brows knit, and he shook his head.

The old man closed his eyes and groaned. "Blast!"

Suddenly, *Señora* Inez screamed.

Clint looked up as Bratcher suddenly appeared in the hallway door, gun in hand. Surprised, the killer jerked to a halt when he saw Clint. A sneering grin curled his thin lips when he saw Clint's six-gun was holstered. He dropped into a crouch and started fanning his .44.

As the .44 boomed, Clint shoved Cooper to one side and threw himself to the other, drawing his Colt while in mid-air and squeezing off three rapid shots as he hit the floor. The last one caught the gunfighter in the chest.

Bratcher stumbled back against the wall, his teeth bared in a vicious snarl. He lurched forward, staggering on legs that were growing weaker. "You—you—"

Clint pumped two more eighty-grain slugs into Bratcher's chest.

Bratcher's eyes grew wide with a look of surprise, and then the snarl on the slender killer's face crumpled into an agonizing grimace. He staggered to a halt, staring in disbelief at Clint. His arm dropped to his side and the Remington .44 slipped from his fingers, clattering on the floor. His lips moved slowly, trying to form words. "Not like this," he muttered, and then his eyes rolled up in his head, and he fell backward to the tile floor.

Clint started to rise, but searing pain burned his side. A guttural groan sounded from deep in his throat as he grabbed at it and pulled away a bloody hand. Clenching his teeth against the pain, he struggled to his feet, and despite his protests, Cooper and *Señora* Inez put him on a bunk where she tended the wound after which she gave him a mug of hot tea steeped from the wild lettuce.

"To help the pain," she said.

"At least, it didn't bust or break no bones. Went clean

through." Eyeing the bandage on Clint's side, Cooper grinned. "Reckon if a man has to get hisself shot, that's the proper place to do it."

Clint nodded, growing drowsy from the soothing properties of the lettuce tea. "Faber? We get him?"

Cooper's grin faded. "No. He got away with three or four of his hired killers. We caught two, killed the others, but Faber got away."

Muttering a curse, Clint tried to sit up, but the last few days of little sleep, of constant stress, and the sedative in the wild lettuce tea had sapped his strength.

Señora Inez gently pressed him back into his bunk with her hand on his chest. "Rest, *Señor* Cleve. *La mañana,* she is time enough."

Chapter Thirty

During the night, *Señorita* Louisa Maria Consuela Cooper arrived and promptly took over the task of tending her brother.

When *Señora* Inez protested, Cooper grinned and waved her away. "You done good, *Señora*. Let the girl look after—" he paused, having noticed a look in his daughter's eyes he had only seen once, and that was in the eyes of his wife when she looked at him. He was going to say, her brother, but instead, he said, "Clint."

Señora Inez looked at him in puzzlement, but when she saw the grin on his lips and the smile in his eyes, she nodded. *"Si, el Patron. Si"*

Clint awakened the next morning with a ravenous appetite. He grimaced against the pain in his side as he rolled out of his bunk. Gingerly, after donning his John

B, he slipped into his trousers and boots, then tucked his blue cotton shirt in and strapped on his pair of .36s.

In the salon, when Maria saw him, she threw up her hands and exclaimed. "*Mi Dios*! You must go back to bed. You are too ill to be up."

Seated at the ponderous table, Cooper grinned at Clint and shook his head.

"Don't worry. I'm fine." Clint laid his hand gingerly on his side. "It's healing good. Whatever the *Señora* dabbed it with is doing good." He pointed to the table. "What I need now is a cup of coffee thick enough to float a horseshoe and a plate heaped with meat and tortillas." He paused, then added, "If you don't mind, *mi hermana.*"

Maria blushed at the reference that she was his sister. At the same time, the familial reference disturbed her, but she could not explain why.

As soon as Maria went into the kitchen, Cooper's smile faded into a grim frown. "You ain't planning on going after Faber, is you? There ain't no need now. We got the place back, and with you here, this time we can hold it."

Clint studied his father, noting how the years had aged the older man. He wished he had returned sooner. Maybe the problems around El Jardin would not have escalated to the present circumstance. "Men like Rawlings and Faber won't quit until they're pushing up grass. We can't cash out of the game now. Give them a chance, and they'll find a way to out-slick us. There're like all greedy men who figure profits from the hard work of others belong to them. We got them on the run, Pa." He shook his head. "Besides, Faber knows who I am now. First thing he'll do back in El Jardin is to notify the Territorial Marshal's office."

The stunning news drove a pitchfork into Sam's belly. Since his son's arrival, he had hoped that he could stay, that they could run the ranch together, that the years past could be forgotten. But, now that Faber knew the truth, Clint would be on the run again, this time, maybe forever.

He closed his eyes and shook his head slowly. Blast them all to hades and back. It wasn't fair. Clint had been dead once, then he returned. To Sam the return of his son was a miracle. And then, the gun wound last night. Another couple inches to the left, and he would have died.

Twice his son had been returned to him. But now, if Clint rode into El Jardin, there was no way on God's Earth he could escape death, the third time. Cooper, leaned forward and laid his hand on Clint's arm. "Best thing you can do is ride out of here now, Son. Get out while you can."

Clint studied the old man. He smiled, and the smile had a touch of irony in it. "The way things look now, I reckon I'm going to have to keep on running, Pa, but I promise you, them two won't be here to cause you no more trouble."

Cooper ran his gnarled fingers through his white hair and pursed his lips. His eyes grew hard. "Me and my boys, we're riding with you."

A faint smile ticked up one edge of Clint's lips, but quickly faded as the realist in him recognized the inherent flaw in a body of men with what he had in mind.

"No. Faber will have guards out. I figure one or two of us can slip in at night and make our play, but they'll spot a passel of riders. It don't make sense to get a dozen family men killed doing a job one gunhand like me can do. Besides, Pa, if you got involved in it, then that would put you on the other side of the law. You'd be running just like me." He gestured to the *hacienda*. "Look what you have here. Look at the people who depend on you. What will happen to them if you turn owl-hoot?"

Cooper studied his son a moment, then nodded. "All right. Do whatever you think is best."

Clint paused, formulating the plan he had in mind. "Here's what I want you to do."

Chapter Thirty-one

Thirty minutes later, Luiz stopped outside the feed room and nodded for the guard to open the door. He held a small bundle wrapped in oilcloth. "*El Patron* sent food for the *gringos.*"

When the door swung open, Luiz tossed the bundle on the floor at the feet of the two cowboys. "Eat. If I had my way, you *gringos* would starve before we hang you tomorrow for the death of *el Patron's* son, Cleve Bollinger."

The guard, Agustin, looked around in surprise. "*Señor* Cleve? He is dead?"

"During the night," Luiz replied, his voice flat and his eyes cold.

The faces of the two hired killers paled. The bald one with the gray-shot beard swallowed hard, and the other closed his eyes and sagged back against the wall.

Luiz stepped back and closed the door, deliberately leaving it unlocked. The guard started to protest, but the lanky ramrod held his finger to his lips and in an unnaturally loud voice said, "Saddle two horses. I must see *el Patron* before Diego and I leave." He glanced over his shoulder at the feed room, then gestured for the guard to accompany him to the stable door that opened outside the compound.

The guard frowned, but did as he was told.

At the door, Luiz whispered. "Do not try to stop the *gringos* from escaping, Agustin. Tell the others."

Agustin opened his mouth to protest, but Luiz shook his head and said, "*El Patron* wishes it so."

As soon as the door closed, the two cowboys jumped to their feet. Baldy whispered, "I don't know about you, Pipkin, but Bratcher didn't pay me enough to stay here and get myself hung."

Pipkin grunted as he tested the shuttered window for the tenth time. "Me neither."

"What about the door? Think we can raise the locking bar?"

Without replying, Pipkin tiptoed to the door. He laid his hand on it, and to his surprise, it moved with a faint groan. He looked around in disbelief. "Them greasers forgot to lock it. Come on."

"Watch out for the guard."

"He's saddling horses."

"Maybe they got another guard out there."

With an impatient snort, Pipkin growled softly, "We

ain't going to find out by not looking. I'm going out."
He opened the door wide enough to peer around the
corner. To his surprise, the stable was empty, and two
saddled horses stood by the hitching rail just outside
the stable door.

Without a word, the two hired killers leaped into the
saddles and headed out for El Jardin.

From the north tower, Luiz watched. A satisfied grin
played over his lips when he saw the two round the corner of the compound and sprint their ponies across the
valley. Just the way *Señor* Clint had planned it.

Later in the salon, Sam stared across the table at
Clint, who was slumped in a heavy chair in front of the
adobe fireplace, his eyes fixed on the Regulator clock
on the mantel. At two minutes before noon, Luiz entered and nodded to Clint.

Wincing from the wound in his side, Clint rose.
"Ready? If we leave now, it'll be dark when we get
there."

The angular *vaquero* nodded. "*Si.*" He glanced at
Cooper who was watching Clint with worried eyes.

At that moment, Maria entered, her face drawn with
concern. "You are foolish to attempt such a thing," she
said. Her black eyes gazed at his side. "The ride will
open the wound."

He grinned at her wryly. "*Señora* Inez did well with
the wound. And the ride will not be hard." He smiled
down at her, filled with a mixture of strange feelings, surprised at the sudden regret he felt in leaving her behind.

She laid her hand on his arm. "Take care of yourself."

Clint nodded. "I will."

Her eyes glistened. "We'll be waiting here for you."

Suddenly, Clint didn't want to leave, but there was no choice. And when he left, he knew he would not be coming back. As far as Clint Bowles was concerned, he would cease to exist once he rode from the *hacienda*, and Cleve Bollinger would be reborn. "Keep the coffee hot," he replied, glancing briefly at Sam who was looking at him with sad eyes.

Clint tried to keep his thoughts focused on Faber and Rawlings during the ride to El Jardin, but the image of Maria kept intruding his thoughts. Finally, he gave in and dreamed of what could have been, and what would never be.

Pipkin and Baldy reached El Jardin in mid-afternoon

Sheriff Hitch Faber stared at the two hired guns in surprise, then pleasure. "You see the body?"

Behind him cleaning the cells, a young Mexican woman glanced up.

Curly shook his head. "Nope. We was locked up in the feed room. We couldn't see nothing, but they was planning on stretching our necks in the morning."

"That's right, Sheriff. That greaser said Bollinger died last night."

Faber leaned back in his chair and studied the two men. A broad smile played over his square face. He rocked forward and pulled a bottle of whiskey from a desk drawer. "This calls for a drink." He turned the bottle up and chugged several gulps, then tossed it to Pipkin and rose to his feet. "I'll be back later," he announced.

Twenty minutes later, Sheriff Faber knocked on the door of Rawlings' *hacienda* and was shown into the study where the businessman was entertaining Judge J B Hyde. Rawlings grinned with satisfaction and nodded to Judge Hyde as the sheriff gave them the news of Bollinger's death. "That means there is nothing to prevent us from going out there and taking the place back. And this time," he added, giving Sheriff Faber a chilling look. "This time, nobody will run us off." He paused. "The judge here tells me that our attorneys have just about worked all of the flaws in the land title for Cooper's place. Isn't that right, Judge?"

The rotund man nodded briefly, cleared his throat, and replied. "Yes. In fact, with what I have, we can take it away from him legally though that would take considerably more time."

"Which I don't have to spare," Rawlings growled.

Faber grew serious. "You know the federal marshal will be here in a day or two."

Rawlings' brows knit. "Federal marshal? Oh, the messenger you sent up to Santa Fe telling them Cleve Bollinger was still alive." He grimaced. "What about sending another messenger saying Bollinger was dead. Would that keep him from coming?"

"No," the judge replied. "Let him come. Let him see we're following the law."

Faber frowned. "What happens when he talks to

Cooper and the others? He might not think things are so law abiding."

Rawling's grin grew wider. "I've already thought of that. How many men can you have ready to ride tomorrow, Sheriff?"

"As many as we need."

"Five or six will be enough."

Faber's frown deepened, and Rawlings explained. "Cooper can't talk if he isn't around. And nobody will believe the jabbering of a bunch of greasers. I just got in a shipment of dynamite. Take a couple cases and blow them out."

"But, the *hacienda*."

"We'll rebuild, bigger and better."

Faber grinned.

Rawlings continued, "Pack the dynamite in your office tonight, Sheriff. I'll meet you there in the morning around ten. Have your men there."

Chapter Thirty-two

The stars glittered with an icy luster in the dark skies. The night was still, the only sound was the crunching of hooves on the crusty snow layering the road, and the soft grunts of the ponies as they breathed out frosty puffs of air.

The soft whistle of a thrush cut through the frigid air, a series of several pure notes, each rising to a crescendo, then fading away.

Clint reined up. "A friend," he whispered to Luiz as a shadow emerged from the forest.

It was Ojo. "It is good to see you, old friend." Clint glanced past him. "I do not see Strong Swimmer."

"Dead. By the hand of the one who worked for those you seek. I go with you."

Luiz made the sign of the cross when he recognized

the newcomer as Apache. Clint assured him. "Do not worry yourself. Ojo is our friend."

The *vaquero* looked at Clint sharply, then fixed his eyes warily on the Apache warrior. Two hundred years of animosity between his people and the Apaches spoke much louder than a *gringo's* assurance. He nodded. "As you say."

An hour later, Luiz pointed into the darkness before them. "Beyond that ridge is El Jardin. We leave road here."

Clint nodded silently and fell in behind the wiry *vaquero*. Ojo Blanco brought up the drag.

Some time later, they reined up, staring down upon the small village sprawling at the base of the ridge they stood on. "My cousin, Platon, lives there," said Luiz, pointing to a cluster of small buildings on the western side of the small town. "Come."

They wound down through the pine and fir. When Luiz turned down a narrow *calle*, Clint glanced over his shoulder. Ojo Blanco had vanished. A few moments later, the *vaquero* reined into a narrow passageway between two stone buildings. In the rear was a small barn and corral.

Silently, the *vaquero* dismounted and slid the rails back so they could enter. At that moment, a door creaked open and from the shadows came a voice. "*Parada. Que va?* Halt! Who goes?"

Luiz whispered, "It is I, cousin Luiz. Quick. Close the corral."

The young Mexican did as he was told. He glanced up at Clint as he hurried to slide the rails back in the posts.

While they saddled the horses in the barn, Luiz explained they needed a place for the night. In the darkness, Platon peered up at the shadow of the large man rubbing down his horse. He muttered a soft exclamation, "Bollinger!"

Clint grabbed his Colt, but Luiz snapped. "Quiet! No one must know."

The smaller man shook his head emphatically. "Do not worry, cousin. I tell no one that Bollinger is here."

Clint studied the dark shadows of the barn and corral suspiciously, his finger tightly against the trigger. Luiz asked the question on Clint's mind. "How do you know Bollinger?"

"I do not, Cousin. Isleta, my *hermana*, my sister, hear two *gringos* tell the sheriff that Bollinger is dead, but when I see the beard and the scar on the face of the one with you, I know Bollinger is not dead."

In the darkness inside the small dwelling, Platon lit a tiny candle and placed it in the middle of the table. He set out bowls of meat and a plate of tortillas along with three mugs of *pulque*.

The excitement in the young man's eyes was evident even in the dim light of the small candle. "We hear of the fight at *el Patron's hacienda*." He looked up at Clint. "We have much love for *el Patron* even after he leave us. Often, he would send his people to look after our ill." He paused. "Then the sheriff and the one named Rawlings come. *Señor* Cooper must flee for his life."

He shook his head. "No, do not worry yourself, *Señor*. No one will know our secret."

Clint slept but little the remainder of the night, his head filled with what could have been. Finally, he dozed, and slept the fitful sleep of one resigned to his fate.

Next morning, Luiz studied Clint across the breakfast table. "What do you plan, *Señor?*"

Clint sipped his coffee. During the early morning hours, he had finally come to grips with the finality of his decision. With the icy calm of a gunfighter, he looked deep into the *vaquero's* eyes. "I'm not certain, but I reckon I'll know when the time is right."

At that moment, Platon hurried in and spoke rapidly to Luiz, glancing at Clint from time to time and pointing to the east.

Luiz nodded and turned to Clint. "Perhaps *Dios* smiles on you, *amigo*. Rawlings is to be in the sheriff's office this morning at ten A.M."

Clint stroked his heavy beard. "Could be you're right, *amigo*. Could be you're right." Suddenly, he paused, remembering how Platon had come to recognize him, the beard and the scar. He rose quickly and rummaged through his saddlebags. He could do nothing about the scar, but he could take care of the beard. Perhaps a clean-shaven jasper wouldn't draw near the attention of a bearded one, especially if the bearded one was Cleve Bollinger.

Just before ten, Luiz accompanied Clint to the barn where he saddled his pony. He gave the cinch one last jerk and fastened it. He turned to Luiz, realizing with a hollow emptiness in his chest that his was the last time he would ever see his father's right hand man. He offered his hand. "Take good care of Pa. Tell him I'll write."

Somberly, Luiz took the proffered hand. "*Si, Señor* Cleve. I do as you say."

With a final nod, Clint swung into the saddle and pulled his pony around.

He sat stiffly in the saddle as the sorrel clip-clopped down the cobbled streets. He reined up two doors down from the sheriff's office and dismounted. He squatted with his back against the wall of a small shop, rolled a cigarette, and waited.

At precisely ten A.M., a carriage rattled up in front of the sheriff's office and two well-dressed businessmen stepped out. They entered the office, the shorter, more rotund one tagging after the taller man.

Clint rose, flipped his cigarette into the street, turned on his heel, and disappeared down a passageway between two buildings. In the alley, he hurried to the rear door of the jail. He tested it. It opened silently, just as Platon had promised it would.

Just as he started to step inside, a guttural voice stopped him. "Hold it right there, cowboy. Throw up them hands, or you're a dead man."

At that moment, two miles east of town, Sam, with Maria riding at his side despite his protests, and fifteen *vaqueros* armed with the weapons of dead *gringos*, rode hard.

After hours of soul searching, Cooper made up his mind that the time to fight back had come. Fight back, and then let the law come to terms with what it had created.

Clint froze.

"All right, now get inside, and don't try nothi . . ." There was a thump followed by a gagging sound.

Clint spun. Eyes bulging in disbelief, a grizzled cowpoke was clutching his neck through which a three-foot arrow protruded. Glancing around, Clint spotted Ojo Blanco on the roof of a nearby adobe. When the old warrior saw Clint, he nodded then vanished.

Clint turned back to the jail. He peered inside the room. It was the cellblock, and to his relief, all the cells were empty. From the front office came a murmur of voices.

Above the murmur, an angry voice exclaimed, "Where are the others? You said they would be here!"

Clint peered through the barred window in the door separating the cellblock from the office. The tall, well-dressed man from the carriage was berating the sheriff. Rawlings, Clint guessed.

The rotund businessman stood behind Rawlings. Deputy Scruggs stood to the sheriff's side.

Faber's face was tight with anger. "I told you they'd be here, Rawlings. So, just calm down."

Clint tugged gently on the door. It moved easily. He drew a deep breath.

Rawlings glared at Faber. "I'll calm down when I'm good and ready."

In one quick move, Clint jerked the door open and stood facing the four surprised men. "Hello, Faber," he growled.

Rawlings frowned. "Who . . ."

Faber's face contorted in rage. "Bollinger! Blast you!" He grabbed leather.

At the same time, the front door swung open and two cowpokes stepped in. When they saw Clint, they grabbed for their six-guns.

Clint dropped into a crouch, fanning off two shots before Faber cleared leather. The slugs punched two holes over the sheriff's heart. Teeth clenched, Clint turned the muzzle on Rawlings, but a heavy force slammed into his shoulder and spun him into the cell block.

In the next second came a deafening explosion, the concussion from which blew the walls out of the office.

A stray slug had struck the cases of dynamite.

Chapter Thirty-three

From somewhere deep in the dark recesses of Clint's brain, tiny electrical impulses began flickering. His eyelids fluttered. Slowly he opened his eyes, but all he could see was complete darkness.

He lay still, becoming aware of the tightly wrapped bandage about his shoulder. He touched a finger to his shoulder and grimaced. At least he was still alive. If he'd been dead, his shoulder wouldn't have hurt.

Gingerly, he moved his other limbs. Nothing seemed broken. He tried to remember what had happened in the jail, but the last conscious thought he had was being slammed to the floor by a slug.

So, where in the Sam Hill was he?

Suddenly, the door opened and a rectangular patch of light fell across the floor. Maria stood in the open doorway, holding a candle. When she saw Clint was awake, she uttered a cry of happiness and hurried to him. Setting the candle on the bench next to the bunk, she laid the back of her fingers on his forehead and nodded. "Good." She straightened and smiled down at him. "Don't worry, you will live."

"Wh—where are we?"

At that moment, another young *señorita* brought her a cup. Maria lifted Clint's head. "Drink. It will help you sleep. I'll answer all your questions in the morning."

For a moment, Clint struggled to sit up, but he had lost much blood, and he was weak. Wearily, he lay back on the pillow, too exhausted to argue.

The sun was high overhead when Clint awakened next morning. The night had been cold, and the door to his room had been left open to allow heat from the fireplace, to warm him. As he lay staring into the salon, voices came to him.

"Where is the marshal, Father? Has he gone?"

Sam's gravelly voice replied, "Yep. Headed back to Santa Fe ten minutes ago. Said he's glad it's all over."

Maria peered into Clint's room. When she saw he was awake, she hurried in and lit a lantern. Sam followed her. "Well, see you decided to join the living." He growled with a grin.

Clint threw his legs over the side of the bunk and sat up. "You said something about the marshal."

Sam winked at Maria. "Yep. He's done come in, looked things over, and decided to head on back. He figured he ain't got no business in El Jardin since it's now being run by an honest and trustworthy man."

The old man laughed at the confusion on Clint's face. He touched a finger to his own chest. "You're looking at El Jardin's new *alcalde*, Clint, Mayor Sam Cooper, elected by the good citizens of El Jardin in a special election upon the death of the previous *alcalde*, the honorable John Rawlings."

"Rawlings? What happened to him? I know about Faber. What happened to Rawlings?"

Sam pulled up a chair facing the bed. "You been out for over two days. The explosion. Best we figure, someone's bullet hit some dynamite and it blew the jail apart, killed every jasper in there except you. Only reason it didn't get you was you was back in the cellblock and them iron bars kept the roof from caving in on you."

He paused, then continued. "As soon as we found Rawlings' worthless carcass, the citizens elected me *alcalde*."

Maria broke in, "That night after we dug you out and buried the others, Marshal Kenton from Santa Fe rode in looking for Cleve Bollinger."

Clint frowned up at her, then turned to Cooper. "So, you lied to him, huh?"

With an expression of supreme innocence on his face, Sam shook his head. "No, Sir. You know me, Boy. I never lie."

Clint looked up at Maria. She smiled mischievously. "He speaks the truth. He, nor any of us in El Jardin, spoke no lie."

"So? Why did the marshal leave?"

"Why do you think?" Sam snorted. "I suppose he figured Cleve Bollinger was kilt in the explosion with the others."

Shaking his head in exasperation, Clint growled, "Would one of you tell me just what in the blazes is going on here?"

Cooper glanced up at Maria. "He able to travel?"

She shook her head. "Not on horseback."

"What about a carriage?"

"*Si.*"

Ten minutes later, the carriage pulled up in the small, neat cemetery on the outskirts of El Jardin. Maria, at Clint's side, pointed to a roughly hewn marker, of wood. "There. That is why the marshal rode back to Santa Fe."

Clint's eyes grew wide as he read the marker.

Cleve Bollinger, b-1839; d-Nov 3, 1868.

He looked around at her. "But the people in town. They know the truth."

She shook her head and took his hand in hers. "No. They are as I. They know that Cleve Bollinger is dead, and that Clint Bowles lives. This is the grave they dug, a grave for a dead gunfighter."

Sam nodded. "She's right. It was the town what come up with the idea. Reckon they figured that someone with guts enough to stand up for them was too valuable a gent to be dangling from a noose."

Clint tried to swallow, but the lump in his throat refused to budge. Cooper cackled, and popped the reins on the horse's rump. "What do you say we get a good night's sleep and then head back to the *hacienda*?

Maria squeezed Clint's hand, and he smiled down at her. "I'd like that real good."

That night as he lay in his bunk staring at the darkness above, he whispered softly, "Well, Speck. You were wrong about one thing. Looks like I did have a little luck left." His eyes filled with tears. "I just wish you and Amy could have had some of it, but don't you worry none. I'll go see her for you."